The Countess Caper

The Dainty Devils
Book 2

By Alyxandra Harvey

Text by Alyxandra Harvey
Cover by Dar Albert

Dragonblade Publishing, Inc. is an imprint of Kathryn Le Veque Novels, Inc.
P.O. Box 23
Moreno Valley, CA 92556
ceo@dragonbladepublishing.com

Produced in the United States of America

First Edition October 2023
Trade Paperback Edition

ARE YOU SIGNED UP FOR DRAGONBLADE'S BLOG?

You'll get the latest news and information on exclusive giveaways, exclusive excerpts, coming releases, sales, free books, cover reveals and more.

Check out our complete list of authors, too!

No spam, no junk. That's a promise!

Sign Up Here

www.dragonbladepublishing.com

Dearest Reader;

Thank you for your support of a small press. At Dragonblade Publishing, we strive to bring you the highest quality Historical Romance from some of the best authors in the business. Without your support, there is no 'us', so we sincerely hope you adore these stories and find some new favorite authors along the way.

Happy Reading!

Kathryn Le Veque

CEO, Dragonblade Publishing

Additional Dragonblade books by Author Alyxandra Harvey

The Dainty Devils Series

The Duchess Games (Book 1)
The Countess Caper (Book 2)

The Cinderella Society Series

How to Marry an Earl (Book 1)
How to Marry a Duke (Book 2)
How to Marry a Viscount (Book 3)

Society isn't ready for this Marriage of Convenience.

Lady Tessa Kilkenny has secrets.

Her ramshackle manor house is filled with mice and snakes and peeling wallpaper—but it's also filled with women with nowhere else to go. Women fleeing husbands, greedy parents, failed love affairs. And Tessa will do anything to keep them safe.

Even steal a carriage from Roarke Noble, the Earl of Dartmoor.

As her first foray into being a highwaywoman, it has mixed results. She gets her cousin to the midwife just in time. But she also gets a marriage proposal.

Because Roarke needs a wife.

And with Tessa he gets more than he bargained for. He married to fulfill a promise, and he has no intention of falling in love with his wife, despite the attraction that sizzles between them, threatening both of their plans. Theirs is a marriage of convenience.

Even if she is particularly inconvenient.

She won't tell him why she is fighting off housebreakers and stealing from earls and viscounts. Or why her disaster of a house is rigged with traps to discourage unwanted visitors. Why there are women hiding behind the furniture.

But when those secrets put her life in danger, Roarke discovers he will do anything to save her.

Note: This series is part of Dragonblade's Flame line, so this is a sexy, steamy, and scorching-hot read with multiple sex scenes. Be advised.

Chapter One

On the last Wednesday of September, Lady Tessa Kilkenny stole a man.

She didn't mean to.

But she wasn't giving him back.

At least, not yet. There simply wasn't time. She needed his carriage, and he happened to be inside of it. That was his own bad luck and nothing to do with her.

Mostly.

Anyway, he would survive. Her cousin Dove might not.

And to think that this time last year she had been sitting down to another interminable tea, her ankles crossed, her gloves pristine, her smile polite and as sweet as the teacakes being served. She had told stories, played the pianoforte when asked, laughed when appropriate, murmured when necessary, her spine straight no matter how tired she was.

She'd survived it with another of those terrible smiles because it was meant to protect her, to make her family love her. She was a lark, always up for a laugh. It was meant to save her cousin Deirdre from ruin, and so much worse.

When it did neither, what, as a woman, was she to do?

Burn it all down.

Metaphorically, of course. She would never damage a three-hundred-year-old house with better bones and a better reputation than anyone in her life. Than herself, come to that. Her reputation had *not* improved. Not to mention Mayfair, with its cobbled stones and marble pillars, would be a bit of work to burn, to be honest.

Still, The Incident followed her.

A week later, a month later. A year later.

And she wasn't the least bit sorry for it.

Lord Tewksbury got what he deserved. He deserved far worse, but she had acted on impulse with the tools at hand.

And now here she was.

Ruined. Banned from Society. Disdained.

And stuck in a thunderstorm with her cousin crouched in the mud, shouting obscenities.

As one of Tessa's first forays into being a highwaywoman, it left something to be desired. But she could hardly be held responsible for Dove's situation. Or the timing of babies deciding they were ready to fling themselves into the world. If she was, she'd have chosen a much warmer day, and a much closer proximity to a midwife. Any midwife, but preferably Noni from the village, which was an hour's walk away.

She didn't know the first thing about childbirth.

Neither did Dove, regrettably. She went by Marigold now, changing her name as they all did when moving to Magpie House. It was safer that way. Only Tessa kept her name because she was not in hiding. And no one was looking for her. Certainly, no one wanted to find her.

Dove—Marigold—hadn't even realized the night she spent with a viscount could result in a pregnancy. Her parents could choke on their indignation and embarrassment. They kept their daughter ignorant and handed all of the power to an unscrupulous viscount who would choke on something more than shame the very moment Tessa found him. He'd pay dearly, both figuratively and literally.

And now here they were, waiting for said viscount, so that Tessa could threaten him with her pistol and steal all of his coins.

She planned to shoot at the sky very dramatically if he pressed her. Babies were expensive. Marigold should be in her rickety bed at Magpie House with her feet up, but she had insisted on coming along, just so she could spy from the bushes to watch him squirm and sputter.

The viscount had yet to make an appearance. Instead, Marigold was the one squirming. And panting. And holding on to a tree while seething with curse words. Her cheeks went from pale to red and back to pale.

"I love you," Tessa said. "But I can't boost you into the saddle. It would be like lifting a whale."

"I'm going to punch you for that remark, Tessa Kilkenny." Marigold made a strange sort of sound and clutched her belly. "Later."

"Do not have this baby in the lilac bush before I get back," Tessa ordered her.

"Hurry."

Tessa paused, momentarily undecided. She didn't want to leave her alone. But they needed a midwife. And a carriage to get there. "Bollocks."

"That's what got me into this situation in the first place." Marigold had spent the last seven months learning everything she could about human anatomy. About illness and medicine and childbirth. About truly disgusting things Tessa would have preferred never to know about.

"True enough."

"Just go," she grunted.

Tessa swung into the saddle, made so much easier by her stolen breeches. She had created an alter ego whose name was Acton. He was very capable. He could find a carriage through sheer luck. In the dark. With a single boot and no hat. A little storm would never stop him.

Tessa, unfortunately, would have to steal a carriage from the first person she encountered or else from the coaching inn nearby. She had breeches, her fairly inaccurate pistol with a single shot, and a rusty antique dagger she had found in the attic.

What could go wrong?

The busy road, usually clotted with traffic traveling to and from the Cornish coast, was deserted.

Of course it was.

The sky, which had started out clear and bright, was darkening rapidly. Rain would soon follow.

"Bollocks," she muttered again. She was not going to let Marigold give birth alone in the mud.

The coaching inn came into view, on the crest of the next hill, wind-stunted trees standing sentinel. The smell of wood smoke and stables whipped down toward her. A single fat raindrop hit the tip of her nose. She pointed at the gray clouds. "Absolutely not."

The stable yard was empty, with only hay under her boots as she dismounted and a sullen stable hand poking his head out. Behind him, shining like the sun, was a carriage. It clearly belonged to a nobleman, already hitched with strong horses who looked like they knew how to handle a spot of trouble.

She could absolutely change her name to Trouble.

She would have tried to manage the reins, even having never handled four horses at once. She was deeply, deeply grateful not to have to make the attempt. A coachman already sat up on the bench, waiting for his master.

Tessa lowered her tricorn hat a touch, hoping it shaded her face, and made sure her very distinctly red hair was stuffed up inside. She tossed the reins to the stable hand and pitched her voice low. It only sounded a little bit like she had a mouthful of rocks. "Stable the horse for Lady Delacourt," she ordered him.

The innkeeper's wife knew the code name and would take good care of Foxglove. She had helped her sister once, the same way she was helping Marigold.

To the coachman, Tessa called up, "Your master needs to get me on the road to Fox Hollow. At once."

She threw herself into the carriage before he could question her. She had only her appearance of authority to back her up. This part would have worked much better were she wearing the fine silk gowns of Lady Tessa, the bright, flighty smile that promised a caper. She kept her hand on her pistol. She'd hate to have to stand up through the roof opening to threaten him, but she would do so in a heartbeat. Another raindrop spattered in the dirt.

She landed on the carriage seat, took a deep breath, and then let out a gurgle of a shout, quickly cut off. She could not afford histrionics.

The shadow sitting across from her implied it was a very big man.

Very big.

A large boot touched her own.

Honestly, if the Fates could be just a bit more helpful today…

Apparently not.

"I'm sorry," she said, holding up her pistol. Adrenaline shimmered through her, along with worry for Marigold, but her hand did not shake. She could be proud of that later. "But I don't have time for this."

"I don't much have time for being robbed," came the dry response.

"I'm only borrowing."

There was a pause, an exhale.

"Lady Tessa," the shadow said darkly. "Why am I not surprised?"

How did he know it was her? She hadn't pulled her scarf up, but her hat, her clothes, the gray light from the storm should have been enough. Her hair was hidden. And this was not the Tessa Kilkenny anyone in Mayfair would recognize. She glared at him. He shifted slightly.

She growled. There was no other word for it.

"You."

Chapter Two

HER PISTOL DID not waver.

If anything, her aim improved. Threateningly.

She would rather have stolen the prince himself, the very devil, in fact, than Roarke Noble, Earl of Dartmoor. *The Beast of Dartmoor.* Ridiculous nickname. Almost as bad as the one the *ton* had given her. *Punch Bowl Ophelia.*

"Where have you been?" he demanded.

She blinked, momentarily nonplussed. Of all of the reactions she might have expected, all of the questions, that one would never have made the list. Not in a thousand years. "Pardon?"

He scowled at her. Not at her pistol, but her. "You vanished from Society."

True. But why on earth had he even noticed? She supposed The Incident was still talked about. She sighed. "You hate Society."

"You don't."

He did not look like an earl. He never had. He was too tall, his shoulders too wide, his thighs too thick. He was entirely and annoyingly too handsome with his shock of dark hair, his neat beard. His green eyes, sometimes like moss, sometimes like stone. Not that she'd noticed. And he wasn't wearing a cravat.

"Where's your cravat?" she asked peevishly, even though she had never once given a whit as to whether or not a man was wearing one.

"You are attempting to steal my carriage because I am not wearing a cravat?"

"No, of course not." He made her ridiculous. Always had.

"Then pray tell."

He was lounging. She was threatening him, and he was *lounging*. He didn't even have the decency to be scared. Nervous. Mildly anxious.

Damn the man.

"I need it," she said stubbornly.

"I gathered that much. Tell me where you need to go in such a state, and I'll take you there myself."

She snorted. "I don't need *you*. I need your carriage."

"I'm afraid we are a packaged set."

She motioned with her pistol. "You're really not." Had he recently fallen on his head? Didn't he realize she was threatening him?

Again, not a particularly inspiring start to her highwaywoman career.

Stealing jewelry from ballrooms would have been so much easier. No one would notice until later, and then they'd assume they had been foxed on wine or a clasp had broken. The idea that it might be found somewhere illicit was worse than losing it, and they might never even make a peep. Perfect, really.

But it had been rather a long time since she had been welcomed in a ballroom.

He continued to watch her steadily. She huffed an impotent sigh. "You know I could shoot you, don't you?"

"Lady Tessa, you are not going to shoot me." He raised an eyebrow, implacable as always. "Despite promising to do so for a great many years."

"Just get out," she snapped. "I'm in a hurry."

He did not move.

Well, that wasn't precisely true. He did not *exit* the carriage. He did, however, move with such speed and skill that she did not see him do so—not until he gripped her wrist in his giant hand, pinning it to the window. He squeezed, just hard enough that the pistol dropped, and he caught it deftly with his other hand.

He still had her pinned to the window.

The Beast of Dartmoor. Feared by the ladies and gentlemen of the *ton*.

"Damn it, Dartmoor."

He did not release her. He was taking up all of the extra space, of which there was not an abundance. His knee moved between her legs. There were only inches between his mouth and hers.

What an odd thing to notice.

He smelled like cedar and wood smoke.

She should not care that he smelled like trees.

"Dartmoor, let go."

He didn't, of course. He had never been obliging, and she hardly expected him to start now. Pistol notwithstanding.

"I don't think so," he said quietly. His gaze dropped to her mouth, flickered back to her eyes. She furrowed her brow, trying to look menacing. He was easily twice her size and likely twice her height. She was not tall.

He was very, very tall.

"Why are you out stealing carriages?" he asked. "Which could get you hanged, I might add."

She sighed. She could continue with their usual sharp banter, poke at him, maybe bite his arm to make him let her go, but meanwhile, Marigold was struggling. Alone. Rain started to patter in the courtyard. "My cousin is currently giving birth in a lilac bush."

Roarke blinked. "Pardon?"

"I don't have time to explain. Baby. Storm. Bushes." He had no right to the details. No one did, despite the gossip. Marigold was the daughter of a vicar, and the gossips had come for her with a vicious glee. They had made of her their bread and butter. Moldy bread and rancid butter.

Roarke thumped on the roof. "Drive on!" he called.

She might not have to shoot him after all.

The coachman urged the horses into a walk.

"North on the road and right at the first crossroads. Hurry. Please."

Roarke relayed that information, still holding her wrist. His fingers were warm and steady, but unyielding. She wondered if he could feel her pulse hammering under his thumb. It was adrenaline. Worry. A reaction to the moment. Not him. Never him.

Liar.

They stayed locked in that strange, fraught embrace for a long moment. Her blood didn't seem to mind that he did not care for her. That he always watched her with that inscrutable expression, as if waiting for her to do something absurd.

To be fair, he was not alone in that. People looked at her like that all of the time now.

The carriage rattled them to and fro like peas in a glass, the horses urged into a gallop. He finally released her, as though it took much willpower. He sat back in his plain coat and rough trousers. Didn't he know earls were meant to go about in formal knee breeches and carry enameled, gilded snuffboxes and pretentious lorgnettes? And smell like thick cologne? Not trees and wind and every delicious winter's day.

"I'll have my pistol back, please," she said, instead of any of those things.

He studied it, then carefully disarmed it before returning it to her.

She snatched it back, frowning. "I'll have the bullet back as well."

"As soon as I'm sure you won't shoot it at me."

"So never, then?" she couldn't help but quip.

"Exactly."

She rolled her eyes. "Bullets are not cheap." Or so she assumed. She had found this one in the attic as well. But if the last months had proven anything to her, it was that nothing was cheap. Not bullets, not paper, not flour. Not glue or brocade or paint, all of which was needed in great supply at Magpie House. Along with nails and hammers and wood. And sugar and pickles and stilton cheese. Pregnant women ate *anything*. It was disconcerting to watch.

The carriage took a hard turn. The momentum slid her along the seat, and she braced herself, but not before Roarke used his leg to steady her, pressing on the outside of her own. "Why are you wearing breeches?" he asked, sounding faintly strangled.

She glanced down at the thick fabric stretching across her thighs. She'd forgotten she was wearing them. "Are you shocked?" she asked. Someone who regularly went about without a cravat should not hold opinions on fashion. "You never struck me as the missish type." And it was hardly the most shocking thing she had ever done. Ask Lord Tewksbury. With any luck, he still had punch up his nose.

"I never thought I was," he said wryly.

Wait until he found out she wasn't wearing her stays under the linen shirt and coat.

"And shocked is not the word I would use."

Before she could ask him—demand, in fact—that he elaborate, the carriage rolled to a stop. Tessa scrambled out, not waiting for the coachman to open the door or for Roarke to get out of her way. She nearly sat on his knee like a mistress at the opera.

She might have blushed, for no good reason, if she'd had the time.

He wrapped his hands around her waist—nearly entirely around her; he was that big—and plucked her off, as if she had offended him. He dropped her on the ground and yet still somehow managed to reach Marigold's side first. Marigold scrambled back, then shouted a curse vile enough to burn the hair off a donkey's arse. Did donkeys have hair? Fur, then.

"It's all right," Tessa assured her quickly. "It's only Dartmoor.

He's here to help."

Marigold blinked. The sky abruptly dropped two storms' worth of rain on them. "I don't care if he's the devil himself."

Roarke did not take offense. Or perhaps he did—it was hard to tell. He did not speak much, and he generally looked as though he was utterly fed up with everyone around him. But in a patient way. She did not know how he managed it. A giant, patient, unruffled rock. If the sarsens of Stonehenge ever fell, he could stand in in a pinch.

Thunder rolled as the wind kicked up, as bad-tempered as that donkey with the burning arse fur. A large branch whipped back and then snapped with a resounding crack. Marigold was safe in the bushes.

Tessa was not.

Roarke did not even have the time to shout a warning. Instead, he lunged, grabbing her by the lapels and hauling her out of the way. The branch scraped his arm, ripping his sleeve before it pierced the dirt like a javelin. Tessa's heart bumped against her ribs. Rain spattered off the rim of her hat.

"Get in the carriage!" Roarke shouted at her. He scooped Marigold into his arms and was at Tessa's heels as she darted ahead. They'd left the door open, and the fine embroidered cushions were wet. The coachman was struggling to calm the horses. The rain turned into needles; the wind lashed.

"To Fox Hollow!" Tessa shouted over the storm. "The midwife's house has a red door, just past the church." She clambered inside the carriage. Marigold sprawled across the seat, trying to breathe through the pain. She was shivering. Roarke had already wrapped his coat around her shoulders. Tessa sat next to him.

"Don't worry," she told her cousin with false cheer. "We're nearly there."

Chapter Three

THEY WERE NOT nearly there.

Marigold was going to have a baby on the floor of a carriage between lightning strikes, and Roarke was bleeding through his shirt.

Tessa kept her smile bright, confident.

"You're smiling that smile," Marigold said.

"Which smile?"

"The one that makes you look like you're going to bake my bones into your bread."

"It's *comforting*."

"Not if it's my bones going into the bread."

"This is the smile that got me through three Seasons, I'll have you know." Tessa adjusted the brightness of her smile. "Better?"

Marigold grunted. Tessa took that as agreement. She hovered on the edge of her seat, wondering if she could catch the baby, should it make its appearance. How fast did they come out?

"Not fast enough," Marigold panted, and Tessa realized she had spoken out loud.

Roarke glanced outside. The window was streaked with rain and splatters of mud. "We're nearly there, I'm sure."

Tessa did not believe him.

Marigold glared at her. "So help me, Tessa Kilkenny, if you tell me to hold it in, my baby and I will both bite you just as soon as she grows teeth."

"She, is it?" Roarke asked.

Marigold bared her teeth. "I am sick to death of men."

He nodded solemnly. "I completely understand."

Marigold nodded back. "You may stay." It was a regal acquiescence, despite the fact that it was his carriage in the first place, and when Tessa had first met her, she could not even hold eye contact with a man.

"Don't get too smug," Tessa said. "He doesn't like anyone. He once said people are as flighty as birds, *especially redheads*."

She knew this to be a fact as he had said to her. Near her. *Possibly* she had been eavesdropping at the time, which gave her less of a right to her moral outrage, but as he had said it after declining to dance with her, she had every intention of holding on to her indignation. As a redhead, it was her duty.

Never mind that she had cultivated the air of a flighty songbird on purpose.

"You can't have meant it," Marigold said.

Roarke settled back against the cushions as if they were on a leisurely jaunt. He was so large that his shoulder brushed hers, his thigh pressed against hers. She scowled and scooted into the corner. She'd have to hang half out the window if this continued. She should probably hold her ground. But something about him made her feel too hot and too aware and too cross. They whispered things about this man. Dark things.

They did not dissuade her, and that was worrisome in the extreme. She had never believed the rumors, the gasps of *murder* and *terrified women*.

It was a relief on many levels when the horses slowed, and the carriage rocked to a stop. Marigold's fingers were leaving indentations in the cushions. "I'll bring her in," Roarke said.

Tessa nodded before jumping outside, not bothering to wait for the coachman to bring the step. She raced to the red door, pounding once with her fist.

It opened just as she was about to barge in. Noni raised her eyebrows and reached for an apron hanging on a nearby hook. "Some babies like a storm," she said mildly. "Bring her in."

Noni was a tall Black woman who had moved to England from Uganda, bringing with her a wealth of midwifery knowledge. Why she had chosen a sleepy village in Cornwall was a mystery to Tessa. And a boon. No one would take better care of her friend. And with so little fuss and judgment. The midwife two towns over was in love with a vicar who was full of fire and brimstone.

This was not the first time Tessa had shown up on Noni's doorstep with a lady in need of help. Nor would it be the last, judging by the occupants of Magpie House. When she had bought the run-down house with the last of her money, she knew the rooms would fill quickly. Women did not have many options. There were always jealous mothers, fathers with tempers, lovers with no honor whatsoever. Viscounts and earls and marquesses.

There were always women with no place to go.

The Incident had shown her that.

It was something Tessa had always understood, especially after her mother died when she was five years old, and her father five years later. But The Incident solidified it. Well, everything preceding it.

She hadn't tried to drown a man in a punch bowl for no reason, after all.

She jumped aside when Roarke ducked into the house, carrying Marigold as if she weighed no more than a cat. A wet, spitting cat promising vengeance on anyone who looked in her direction. Noni smiled. "Good afternoon, Marigold."

"I hate this."

"I can see that," Noni said mildly. She was used to women in labor. She was entirely unruffled. Tessa loved that best about her.

Roarke took Marigold into the bedroom Noni pointed out for him. When he returned, Tessa was still standing by the door, water dripping off the brim of her hat. He raised an eyebrow. "Aren't you going to go in with her?"

"No, thank you," Tessa said politely. "Absolutely not." He blinked. She wrinkled her nose. "I am not... sanguine about blood. If you'll pardon the pun."

"But..."

"Would *you* like to go in there and watch the process of childbirth?"

His neck tensed. "No, thank you," he replied, equally politely.

"Ha," she returned, well vindicated. "Then I don't see why I should feel any differently."

She would have said more—a lot more—but Noni's apprentice came through the door, rain dripping from her curls. Beth was short and stout, with a gentle smile that could soothe the fussiest soul. "I saw the fancy carriage," she said. "Oh, Lady Tessa. It's you."

Tessa nodded. "Marigold's just inside."

"Excellent." Beth traded her cloak for a white apron. "Not to fear—we'll have her sorted in three shakes of a lamb's tail."

It turned out Beth was not exaggerating.

In the time it took for Tessa to thank Roarke and send him on his way, Beth went into the room, the door cracked open to the sounds of grunting and swearing, and one choked scream, followed by the wail of a newborn baby, and then she was poking her head back out. "It's a girl."

Tessa grinned. "She knew it would be. Are they...?"

"Perfectly well. You got here just in time, it seems."

Tessa ducked inside to smile at her sweaty, red-faced cousin and her equally red-faced baby. "Look what you did!"

Marigold beamed, proud and exhausted. "I hated every second of that. And it was worth it." Her eyes drifted shut as Beth took the baby and then toweled the rain from Marigold's plait.

"She'll stay here for a couple of days," Noni commanded. "You can fetch her on Tuesday. Maybe Wednesday. I'll send word to the house."

Tessa squeezed her hands. "Thank you." She'd sell something else or steal it between now and then to cover the costs. It wasn't anything she hadn't done before. She intended to send the viscount the bill just as soon as she could. If only she knew someone suitably massive and intimidating to make her point.

Someone like Roarke.

Who was waiting outside.

For her.

"That was quick," he said from inside the carriage as she came out. The rain continued to fall, but the lightning seemed less inclined to seek them out personally.

"It is, sometimes. Although I expect Marigold would punch you for saying so." She frowned at him. "What are you still doing here?"

"I'm waiting for you."

Surprise, an unexpected rush of warmth. Then suspicion. This was Roarke, after all. She had known the earl since her debut, but always at the fringes of conversations. She had been a social butterfly, determined to make everyone at ease around her. She had only managed to entice him into a single grunt in response to her attempts at light conversation. And a remark about redheads, of course.

"Why?" she asked.

"You're not walking home in this monsoon."

She shrugged. "I'm already wet."

He swallowed. "Just get in."

She climbed in, after sighing loudly to be heard over the raindrops on the roof. "There's no need." Not that she had been particularly looking forward to the wet slog through the fields. Her breeches were already sticking to her legs.

Roarke kept his eyes very carefully on her face. Interesting, that.

"I'm heading to Magpie House as it is," he replied.

"It is customary to wait to be invited," she pointed out drily.

"I was invited."

She narrowed her eyes. "To my house."

"Is it your house?" He sounded so innocent, so unruffled.

"Yes."

"Then I suppose so."

"By whom?" she demanded.

"Lady Summer."

Was that curiosity in her belly? Disappointment? Envy?

Neither. It was neither. She was cold and hungry, was all. Nothing a plate of biscuits couldn't fix. And a warm fire.

"She didn't tell you?" he asked.

"She did not."

"Then I apologize for the intrusion."

He'd already done her a favor today and likely saved Marigold. She should be gracious. It had been as easy as breathing not too long ago. "Not at all. We owe you our thanks. I don't know how to repay you."

"I do."

She lifted her eyebrows. "Oh?"

"You could marry me."

She had never been *that* gracious.

Chapter Four

SHE STARED AT him for a full minute when she realized he was not joking.

"You did ask," he pointed out, as if he'd just requested a second cup of tea.

She sputtered. He was teasing her. He had to be.

What an odd jest.

Still, just a jest.

She tilted her head as the carriage pulled in front of the house. "Did that branch hit you on the head? Are you here to propose to Lady Summer?" That made sense. "Because she and I look nothing alike."

What did not make sense was how much she hated the thought.

Loathed it.

In her bones.

Her fickle, treacherous bones.

Never mind that. She had a brain to think with, didn't she? Who listened to their bones, anyway?

He helped her from the carriage without explaining or elaborating. When he paused to survey the house, she knew what he saw: an old manor built of gray stone which badly needed repointing if it could be dug out from the encroaching ivy. As the ivy had won the battle decades before Tessa was born, she did not hold out hope. Not to mention, repointing was likely to be obscenely expensive. Everything about the house was obscenely expensive. Even if it did not look it.

Roarke would expect glittering windows with velvet curtains, gold candlesticks, gleaming parquet floors. What he saw were crumbling chimney pots, a front door that was slightly crooked, the wood swollen in one corner. Windows rusted shut. And inside was so much worse. If the outside resembled a fine old lady fallen genteelly into hard times, the inside was her drunk sister who had set fire to the place before throwing a chamber pot at the local constable.

That was a rather detailed image, even for her. But the house just did that to her. It invited her to imagine all sorts of possibilities with the peeling wallpaper, water stains on the ceilings, birds in the ballroom. A questionable smell in the back parlor.

Roarke, like everyone else, would see an impulsive, foolhardy purchase, at best. Something a pampered debutante might choose because she had no idea how the world worked. Certainly nothing worth going into considerable debt over.

But Tessa saw home. Freedom. Security. Choices.

A haven.

She refused to be embarrassed. Every dream started somewhere. And anyway, she had not invited Roarke to poke holes in her dreams. She had not even invited him here in the first place.

She pushed at the door. There was no butler, naturally. She had to kick the bottom twice, hard enough that her toes were starting to be tender from the daily abuse. It finally popped open, and she nearly tumbled inside and sprawled on her face. Her elbow tingled, ready for the hard introduction to the floor. It knew from experience. Only this time, a large hand caught the back of her coat and held her steady. The abbreviated fall made her stomach tilt.

Roarke still had not spoken. He merely followed her inside. She sighed at the mess gathering under their feet and wondered what he would say if she made him take off his boots. It was tempting, but she couldn't ask him to risk splinters and gangrene from the state of the floors. They were clean, but in terrible shape. And everything tilted north. It was a bit disconcerting before you got used to it.

Roarke, naturally, did not look disconcerted. Boulders never did.

Lady Summer, twin sister to the Duke of Tremaine, joined them from the only usable parlor. "There you are," she said. "Where's Marigold?"

"Lying in with her daughter." Tessa grinned. "She's named her Parsley."

"Wonderful," Summer said. "Not the name, of course. It's appalling." She reached out to kiss Roarke's cheek. "Well, if it isn't the Earl of Dartmoor."

"You summoned?" he asked drily, but fondly.

"I did." She looked exactly as she should: beautiful, charming, dressed in silk. Her dark hair curled fetchingly. Her smile was bright and welcoming. There wasn't a spot of mud on her, not even any dust in her hair, and Tessa had yet to go an hour in the house without dust or cobwebs or dirt on her face.

Summer looked like a duke's sister.

Tessa did not look like a viscount's daughter.

Or a viscount's cousin, now that George had taken over the estate. Even when she was not wearing breeches. She wasn't about to let it bother her. Summer and Roarke would make beautiful, giant children who barely spoke but glittered like stars.

And Tessa would—

"Tessa!" Holly interrupted from the top of the stairs. She had come to them as Henrietta. Sometimes Tessa worried she would forget her friends' real names, and whispered them to herself. "The attic is turning into the Thames, and we've run out of buckets."

Tessa would battle the leaking roof. Forever.

It was not a bad destiny, truth be told. If she could keep it from crumbling around her.

"We'll use the chamber pots from the extra bedrooms," she called back, starting up the stairs. She avoided the third step out of habit. Everyone avoided the third step. Ankles were delicate, necessary things. Just ask Holly. And Daphne. Her knee was still purple from her last altercation with the third step. "It'll have to do for now."

She paused halfway up, leaning over the banister toward Summer and taking her life in her hands. There was an ominous creak. "His arm needs seeing to."

"It's fine," Roarke said, his voice rolling up her spine, even from a distance. It was probably just her damp shirt.

"You're bleeding on my floor," she pointed out.

He scoffed. Looked down. Paused. "Damnation."

She took the rest of the stairs at a run. Summer could handle his cut, and if she didn't hurry, they might be all washed away before teatime.

Teatime. Tessa had no idea if there was anything decent enough to serve an earl. Blast.

Holly helped her gather the chamber pots, digging them out from under beds that had been covered up for years. Sheets covered chairs, the occasional table. Dust was thick as snow. The house could ostensibly welcome several dozen people. One day. Not currently, clearly. Holly sneezed, as if proving her point. Most of the bedrooms were in shambles.

The attic was an outright mess.

Were she not made of sterner stuff, Tessa might have considered a good cry. A pout. A full-on rage. Instead, she indulged in a single sigh and then slogged through the sodden boxes of old dresses, tarnished silver (they'd missed that box—silver could be sold off for a pretty penny), broken chairs. The floor was disconcertingly soft under her boots. "Careful you don't fall through," she warned Holly as they wove between buckets full of rainwater.

"I'll be careful," Holly promised, hand over her very pregnant belly. "My ankle has just healed."

They hauled the buckets to the one window that opened, mostly because it was broken. A pigeon flapped at their heads in protest. "I know you lived here first," Tessa muttered. "But we live here *now*."

They tossed the dirty water outside, dragged the buckets back into place, and then added the chamber pots under the new leaks. Tessa wiped her hands on her breeches. "That should do it," she said. "Rain's starting to let up, too, so that's a help."

"When the floor gives out, we'll be crushed in our beds," Holly said. She did not sound concerned. She rather liked being morose. Eerie, even. Tessa was used to it. She found it oddly charming.

"Think of the poems they'll write." Tessa patted her arm.

Holly's eyes twinkled. "I would *love* that."

"I know," she said. "You might want to start on one now."

"You know, I think I shall. This house could do with a ghost. Someone bloodthirsty."

"Yes," Tessa agreed wryly. "That's just what we need."

Holly had joined them three months ago, clearly increasing and yet thin from hunger and wary of help. Her sister—Daphne now—had heard that Tessa might help, and they had both landed on the doorstep. Daphne offered to do the gardening in exchange for their room and board. Tessa would have taken them in regardless. Which was a good thing, as the gardens were only slightly less of a disaster than the attic.

Daphne had slightly oversold her talents. Apparently liking flowers was the not same thing as knowing how to grow them. Nor was being a lord's daughter with a team of gardeners. But she *had* managed to save the rosemary and mint bushes, and some of the thyme. And she discovered some carrots and leeks still growing in the corner of the abandoned kitchen garden. At the time, it had felt like a feast.

Tessa was the last to complain. Before buying Magpie House, she'd had no idea how to boil water or bake bread or cook anything at all. She'd never learned. A viscount's daughter wasn't meant to know such things. She was meant to decorate every room she entered like an expensive bauble. A diamond.

A viscount's daughter also wasn't meant to have her inheritance stolen by the next in line for the title.

Damn George, anyway.

She could bake bread mostly without turning it to rock now, boil water for tea with only minimal burns to her fingers. She even knew how to make a decent cottage pie. And keep the slugs off the lettuce.

She did not, however, know how to patch a roof.

Sighing, she changed out of her wet highwayman's costume into a regular dress, dark blue with ribbons at the hem. If she added a spencer with lace points at the sleeves and brushed her hair, it was only because she was accustomed to dressing for guests. Any guests.

Roarke wasn't special.

She'd been telling herself that for ages.

She still didn't believe it.

Chapter Five

It was Tessa who had bounded carelessly up the stairs, but it was Lady Tessa Kilkenny who entered the parlor.

She wore a dress that brought out the fire in her hair, the glint in her eyes. Roarke was more familiar with this version of her, the one who knew how to curtsy, who smelled like roses and amber. He remembered that scent. Dreamt of it, despite himself.

But now that he had seen the other Tessa, the one who gadded about in breeches and stole carriages—he knew he was done for. He'd thought about her more than was likely right even before this moment. Wondered at himself for it. Wondered where she was, what she was doing. When he might spy her through a crowd or in the crush of a ballroom. Where she went when she disappeared from London.

Which, considering he abhorred both crowds and ballrooms, was a feat in itself.

He'd worried for days. Weeks. Only Summer's casual comment that she had just had a letter from Tessa had calmed him.

But this Tessa…this Tessa would break him.

It was not a particularly helpful development. Especially with a marriage offer on the table. He was here because she was unconventional. Not because found her intriguing. If anything, that was a point against her. Whatever strange ribbon connecting them was entirely in his mind. Or, more likely, firmly planted in his lower body. That was to say, nothing she would have felt or noticed. He didn't delude himself. Noticing a sunflower glowing on a gray day did not mean that the sunflower noticed you.

And he knew full well that most people would take his need for solitude personally. He had evidence of that, clearly. He had not been able to keep his wife happy, and she had run off to London within days of their marriage. Which had suited him fine.

What happened afterward did not. Even before the rumors, before ladies paled at his approach, and gentlemen blustered.

But if that need for solitude was preferable, if it was understood from the beginning…

In any event, he was running out of time. His birthday was in less than a week. He loved his mother, but she had made things difficult. He imagined she was even now giggling from some cloud in heaven. Or giggling in hell, which most of her family would assume. He missed her.

Despite this irritation.

"Have you had tea?" Tessa inquired.

Summer, sitting by the fire, snorted. "Rue is in the kitchen at the moment."

"Ah."

Roarke watched them exchange a knowing glance followed by a small shudder. "Is your cook so terrifying?" he asked.

Tessa wrinkled her nose. "We don't have a cook at present, so we all take turns," she explained. "I'm afraid that Rue is by far the most skilled, but she is also the most likely to throw a knife at your head if you interrupt her."

"You don't have a cook?" He'd never known a houseful of wellborn women not to have a full staff. Summer had eaten off gilded plates and drunk from crystal cups every day of her life. As a viscount's daughter and an heiress, he couldn't imagine Tessa was much different. Hell, any earl worth his salt was the same.

He was not particularly worth his salt.

And, to be fair, he couldn't have imagined her in those tight, wet breeches either. He wouldn't be able to stop now. The way they molded to her bottom, to the curve of her strong legs. He didn't think she would mind a long ramble through the moors, climbing the Dartmoor hills and greeting the wild ponies. He could count on one hand the number of people, never mind ladies, who did not think him touched in the head for his preference for the wind over the expensive clatter of silver cutlery and polite chitchat.

Tessa might understand.

Hope he had no business feeling or feeding unfurled inside his chest.

He cursed Summer under his breath. This was a bad idea.

The best idea he'd ever had.

The worst.

"Roarke, are you growling?" Summer inquired.

"Of course not."

Probably.

Definitely.

"I expect you're hungry," Tessa said apologetically. "I'll brave the beast in her lair."

"No need," Summer said cheerfully. She pulled a picnic hamper from behind her chair. "I am prepared. After last time, I didn't want to go to bed hungry again." She lifted the lid to reveal apples, pears, bread and cheese wrapped in waxed linen, jars of almonds and walnuts. Four pots of jams, one of honey.

"What happened last time?" Roarke asked. Everything about today had not gone as expected, and he had known it was going to be an odd day to begin with. Add a theft, tight breeches, childbirth, and hidden refreshments, and he honestly did not know what to expect next.

"We went to bed very hungry," Summer explained. "*Very* hungry. And then Rue woke us at four o'clock in the morning to taste her strawberry crumble."

"It was worth it," Tessa said. "But you are brilliant," she added. "Because Lord Dartmoor might not be hungry, but I could eat a Christmas feast to myself."

"The entire goose?"

"And the trimmings."

Summer grinned, pulling out a roll of bread. "You'll find it's best not to let Tessa get too hungry. She gets a bit feral."

Tessa snatched it from her. "I'm sure I don't know what you mean."

"You nearly bit my finger yesterday."

"You were so *slow*. I've seen snails move faster." She stepped closer, but her foot caught on a loose floorboard. She faltered, and Roarke moved to catch her, but she had already steadied herself, clearly out of long habit. There was a soft rip as the hem caught a loose nail. She sighed. "That's the third time this week."

She would break her neck before the month was out. It filled him with an icy fury. She should have footmen to open doors and maids to bring tea and workmen to fix the bloody floorboards. He cast about for something suitably heavy, settling on an iron poker by the fireplace. He used it to force the nail back down into the floorboard. "This house is a disaster."

Her face immediately pinched in response. Her eyes narrowed; her mouth turned grim.

He'd clearly said the wrong thing.

Again.

There was a perfectly good reason he kept his mouth shut most of the time. He wasn't good at being charming, at throwaway compliments, small chatter. Lies. And it almost always ended like this. With a beautiful woman staring daggers at him.

Summer shook her head. "Oh, you've done it now, Dartmoor." She took a large bite of an apple and sat back, as if waiting for fireworks.

He frowned. Surely the fact that the house was in shambles was not a surprise.

"I didn't say I didn't *like* it," he clarified.

Mollified, Tessa looked less likely to murder him. Bodily harm was still clearly on the agenda, but he could deal with that. She was the size of a mouse.

On the other hand, he might like to arouse her temper.

Poor choice of words. Because he most certainly wanted to arouse her.

He shifted uncomfortably.

Tessa watched them both. She widened her eyes at Roarke. She very much thought she was communicating something. Trouble was, he had no idea what it was. He raised an eyebrow. She motioned her head toward Summer. Twice. As if that cleared things up.

She huffed a sigh. "Did you ask her?" she finally mouthed as Summer turned away to pour lemonade into cups.

"Ask her what?" he said.

She closed her eyes briefly. "I was trying to be subtle."

Summer laughed. "Tessa, you are many wonderful things, but subtle is not one of them."

"Oh, very well," Tessa muttered. "Are you betrothed, then?"

Roarke stared at her blankly. Summer spilled her drink. "What's this now?"

"I'm not here to marry *Summer*," Roarke said. He grimaced at the thought.

"Hey!" she protested at this expression, mostly because she liked protesting.

"Apologies, cousin." He turned to Tessa. "I came to marry *you*."

She blinked. Once. Twice. Three more times. He was about to ask her if she was having some kind of reaction to the dust around the place, then thought better of it.

"I invited him," Summer rushed to add, as if that would make a difference. "You can trust him. He's a good egg."

A good egg.

He nearly growled again.

"If a bit reclusive," Summer added. "And maybe a bit rough around the edges? Some women like that."

He was going to strangle her.

"I was sure I'd misheard you," Tessa finally said. "In the carriage."

"Not at all."

She stared at him for a long moment, then glanced at Summer. Her voice was gentle, excruciatingly polite. "Have you both lost your minds entirely?"

"He needs a wife," Summer said, as if that explained everything. Or *anything* at all.

Roarke rubbed his face. "I am begging you to stop helping."

TESSA FELT AS if she was watching a play on Drury Lane. She'd had strange conversations before. One didn't fill a house with ladies on the run without a surprising discussion or two. Or twenty. To say the least.

But this was something else entirely.

"I don't need a husband," Tessa felt the need to point out.

"You need money," Summer told her. "For this house." She waved her hand, encompassing the general state of things. And she wasn't wrong. She was also mad as ten cats in a bathtub.

Not a metaphor.

As Tessa had occasion to know. Magpie House had come with a dilapidated barn full of peevish occupants.

Tessa couldn't *marry* Roarke. He didn't even *like* her. He just stood around watching her disapprovingly from the corner of ballrooms and museums and muttered about redheads. She knew because she couldn't help but watch him back.

And that was *before* The Incident.

Plus, she'd just abducted him. In her experience, earls frowned upon that sort of thing. Not that she'd abducted anyone *recently*, but they certainly did not like being held up by a highwayman. Or disagreed with at dinner. Ignored. Or mocked, which was usually so much easier.

Drowned in a large crystal bowl filled with claret.

"I'm not sure I like being bartered," Roarke only said mildly.

The women snorted in unison, without an ounce of pity. "Welcome to every day of our lives," Tessa said.

Wisely, he abandoned the protest.

But he stayed where he was, watching her patiently, completely at ease even though he dwarfed the furniture, and she wasn't entirely convinced the spindly antique chair legs beneath him would hold. Dust motes danced in the air around him, like a crown.

"He's kind and does not fuss overly," Summer continued.

"I am starting to feel like a pig at market," Roarke said.

"And he's handsome enough, I suppose," she allowed, ignoring him as only family could. "If approximately ten feet tall and built like an ox. You don't believe that Beast of Dartmoor nonsense, surely. Oh, and he's kind to dogs!"

"Right," he said in his calm, gravelly voice. "That's enough of that."

He rose from his chair and clapped his hands around Summer's shoulders, lifting her bodily off the floor. She squeaked mutinously. It did not deter him one whit. He merely strode across the parlor, deposited her gently in the hall, and then closed the door in her face. And then he locked it for good measure.

"Roarke!" Summer shouted, rattling at the handle. "Let me back in."

"No." He turned to face Tessa, whose mouth had dropped open despite herself. Summer was not often bested. Nor were duke's sisters carted about like a sack of potatoes. "Let's try that again, shall we?"

Chapter Six

"I HAVE TO tell you, Lord Dartmoor, *I* am usually accustomed to being the oddest person in the room."

He smiled briefly. "I am not here to usurp your crown."

"I fear you've already won it," Tessa muttered.

He placed his hands on the back of the settee. It only groaned a little in reply. It was patterned with sleepy-looking quails and was her favorite. She hoped to be able to mend the tear in the fabric by the armrest. "Why do you say you are odd?"

She shot him a look of incredulity. "Are you mocking me, my lord?"

"No," he replied simply.

Since he appeared to be telling the truth, she decided to answer him. It wasn't as if her plans for the day hadn't already unraveled beyond comprehension. "I can pretend well enough," she allowed.

"I've never known you to be anything but charming and vivacious."

"And flighty. Redheaded."

He frowned. "I am sure I never said that."

She snorted.

"Then I am sure I never meant it."

"Never mind—it only proves my point, I suppose." Why should she expect him to magically see through her mask? That was hardly fair.

"Which is?"

"I can host a dinner party and speak three languages while saying nothing of import at all. I can make the most dour and proper of dukes smile. I can dance and I can sing. I can recite a terrifying amount of *Debrett's Peerage* from memory."

"I fail to see the problem."

"I was like a doll. But inside I am too loud and too forceful and too distracted. I always have been." Too much. Always too much. Even her father had said so, and he loved her. The parade of family relations that came afterward were considerably less amused when they made the pronouncement. And that was when she was still trying her hardest to be about as scandalizing as a sugar confection served to an elderly queen.

"Are you now?" He sounded interested instead of repulsed.

"And I occasionally wear breeches, in case you've forgotten." He did not need to know she robbed men of the peerage. Men of his acquaintance. They deserved it. If they would not rise to their obligations, their obligations would hunt them down. She saw to that.

"Believe me, it's not something I will easily forget."

She rolled her eyes. "Yes, yes, I'm sure I offended your delicate sensibilities. Very scandalous. Disgraceful, even."

"If you like." He did not sound scandalized. Interesting.

"And you must know about… Well, The Incident."

"I can hear the capitals in your voice. The sheer melodrama."

She made a face. "I was not the one who called it that. But it stuck."

"It did." He inclined his head. "Lord Tewksbury, was it?"

"Yes."

"Did he deserve it?"

"That and much worse."

He just nodded.

She stared at him. "That's it? You do not care that I dunked an earl in the punch bowl until he choked?"

He shrugged. "I never did like the man much."

She could count on one hand the number of people who had *not* been shocked and horrified by her actions that night. Summer was not even one of them, as she was shocked and horrified that she had missed the show. She mentioned it frequently.

Tessa barely remembered it. It was all rage and wine stains. She did remember passing the alleyway where her cousin had died, all because she was a lady and ladies did not have children out of wedlock. Not marquess's daughters, at any rate. Never mind that her paramour, Lord Tewksbury, who had sworn love and marriage, was still feted as a catch. Doors had closed to Deirdre, and she had run away in a depressive state before Tessa could stop her. Before she could find her cousin, it had all fallen apart in the mud of an alleyway.

When she'd passed that alleyway full of mud and garbage and a stain that looked like blood a week later—something inside of her had snapped.

She had gone straight to the Tewksbury mansion.

Never mind the summer ball in progress.

Never mind that she did not have an invitation.

She marched through the crowd, her hem wet with alley mud, and found him by the punch bowl, serving a debutante not yet eighteen and with stars in her eyes. Tessa had grabbed him by the hair and shoved his face into the wine punch.

She'd been evicted—eventually. Not before he had yelped and sputtered, not before his pristine cravat and coat dripped red, his eyes stung, his hair matted to his forehead.

She'd been evicted from the ball. From her cousin's house. From Mayfair. From the *ton*.

And she would do it again.

Roarke ran a hand over his face. "I admit this was not how I planned to go about this."

"Your marriage proposal."

"Exactly right."

She didn't know what to think. She could not help but wonder if this was some elaborate ruse. "Let's start here, then: why me?"

"You are unconventional."

Right. That.

"I need someone who does not have traditional expectations."

She stared at him. "What does *that* mean, exactly?"

"I need a wife in name only."

"I see." He wanted to marry her because he didn't *like* her.

It just figured.

Not that she should be surprised. Earls did not marry ruined ladies. Even beasts.

He groaned. "I am muddling this up."

She waited. It was silly to feel hurt.

"I promised my mother that I would marry again by my thirty-fifth birthday."

Her eyebrows lifted. "Truly?"

"Unfortunately, yes. It was a deathbed promise because she was very, very clever." He sounded both fond and irritated. Loving. "She was afraid I would be soured against the entire institution because of my first experience."

"The Beast of Dartmoor," she murmured.

"It was a long time ago."

"How long now?"

"Fifteen years."

She sat back. "Oh."

"We were married less than a year. We lived in the same house for exactly one week before she fled for London."

"You did not follow her?"

"She specifically asked me not to. And I hate London. It breaks me out in hives."

"Me too." It hadn't used to.

He looked pleased at that, and then stoic, as if being pleased was against the rules.

Meanwhile, she no longer had any idea of what the rules even *were*. Marriages were often a business arrangement for families like hers, and the Noble family specifically, seeing as Roarke Noble was the Earl of Dartmoor. It was a matter of dowries and estates and little earl babies. She was not naïve.

She was, however, confused.

Her dowry, while substantial, was also fictional. Meaning George had already spent it and would most definitely not offer to replace it. He would not even give her the annuity that was due from her own mother's inheritance, over which he technically had no rights whatsoever. There were legalities involved, and he could afford much better lawyers than she could. Perhaps Roarke did not know that, though. She was not sure if it was common knowledge.

"I do not have a dowry," she said bluntly.

"I did not ask for one." He straightened. "But why do you not have one, exactly? The Kilkenny family is well off, and an old, distinguished name. I've not heard of any insurmountable debts."

She sighed. No, her cousin was cleverer than that. "Do you know George Kilkenny, Viscount Raleigh?"

"Aye," Roarke replied. "He's a right tosser."

She smiled. "He's my cousin."

He winced. "Apologies. Of course he is."

"Not at all. He *is* a tosser. Also, a greedy rat bastard."

"Ah." He cocked an eyebrow. "In charge of your dowry, is he?"

"Aye," she returned, imitating his stern, sharp tone.

His smile was brief, a mere quirk of the corner of his mouth. She rather liked it.

"I'm sure you'd rather not be related to him. And anyway, as an earl you can do much better than me. Any duke or marquess would be glad to have his kin as a countess."

"But not you?"

She frowned. "I don't rightly know." She had been raised to want just that but had not thought about it much recently. Certainly, she could do more for the inhabitants of Magpie House if she were a countess. She might even be able to afford new mattresses. Chairs without splinters. A few burly footmen to help trounce any gentlemen that found them. She quite enjoyed planting a facer, especially to an unsuspecting gentleman of the *ton*, but some of them were quite tall. She'd need a ladder to reach them.

She glanced at Roarke.

"I've had a duke's daughter as a wife," he said. "And I thought she might be happy, that we might be happy in our own way, but..."

"What happened?" She knew enough not to believe the rumors, but not much else.

"She died. In childbirth."

"I'm sorry." She thought of Marigold, and sent up another prayer of gratitude.

"Thank you. It was not my child, but still a wee bairn. She was no bigger than a minute." There was sorrow there, however complicated. "We were strangers, really."

"Aren't we?"

"Not like that. And anyway, you just said you don't want a husband. You're perfect."

She was perfect because she was unconventional. Forgettable. Easy to be around. Easy to leave behind. No demands.

He had no idea how raw the holes in her self-worth were that he was carelessly poking.

Her father had done his best after her mother had died, but then he'd also died too young. And she was sent to live with a string of relatives who foisted her off to the next house as soon as could be.

Marigold's parents said they could not afford to keep her, when Tessa knew it was only that they did not like her influence on Marigold. George's mother resented every single penny and every single ounce of attention that was saved for her son. There were others scattered in between—an elderly spinster aunt who died, a great-uncle who forgot she was living in his house.

"You would have the protection of my name," Roarke continued. "My respect, of course. And two hundred pounds as a monthly income, which, as Summer said, you clearly need for this ramshackle disa—*house*."

That was a *fortune*.

"I see," she said, because she wasn't sure what else to say.

An absolute fortune.

"Say you'll think on it," Roarke murmured.

"You can't afford for me to think on it. You only have a few days, by your own account."

"I can afford one night."

She nodded, but before she could say anything else, a bell rang from the foyer, loud and shrill. Roarke started.

Tessa sighed. "You'll rescind your offer by morning," she said.

He towered over her nonchalantly. "I am made of sturdier stuff."

He was probably used to physically removing obstacles with little effort. Muscles or money, they would see him clear of most problems.

He did not know Magpie House.

Or its inhabitants.

She smiled. She couldn't help it. "Let's see, shall we?"

She wasn't disappointed.

He followed her out of the parlor and down the hall, where Rue rang the bell like a nun spotting Viking ships on the shore. She turned and waved a butcher knife at Roarke. It dripped with what Tessa hoped was the blood of a roast and not a human.

"Who the hell is he?"

Chapter Seven

"RUE, THIS IS Lord Dartmoor." Tessa made the introductions as though they were still in the drawing room and there was nothing at all untoward about being threatened with a dripping knife.

Rue, pink-cheeked and with golden hair that reached down to her elbows in loose curls she never bothered to put up when at home, scowled. "Is he on the list?"

Roarke stood very still, for which Tessa gave him points. Rue was not above stabbing a man in the foyer, earl or no. Actually, the fact that he was an earl was decidedly not in his favor. Rue had not been well treated by an earl. It was all she would say on the matter.

"He's not on the list," Tessa replied. The list was currently tacked to the wall in the kitchen. It was decorated with knife marks and holes left by angry forks. *Lord Tewksbury. Lord Beville. Viscount Eastbourne.* And *Viscount Raleigh*, just so she could have the pleasure of seeing George's name poked through with holes. They'd spent several hours playing very cathartic games of darts in those first few weeks.

"He was invited. He's here for Summer."

"For you," Roarke said quietly.

Tessa refused to feel a flutter. He was *correcting* her, not complimenting her.

The small flutter was not so easily convinced.

Bodies were rather inconvenient when they went against one's logical brain. Tessa's brain knew he had chosen her because he did not particularly care for her.

Her body still wanted to climb him like a tree. That rough voice. Those huge, patient hands. The way he looked down at her with beetled brows as if he knew she was up to some mischief.

Her body liked that. Her thighs, her belly. The pulse in her throat.

Her brain had no time for it. Especially when the possibility of a stabbing was still quite high.

"Is that his carriage?" Rue demanded.

Roarke and Tessa glanced out of the window. "Yes," they replied in unison.

Rue lowered the knife. Slightly.

"The earl is Summer's cousin," Tessa elaborated. "He helped get Marigold to Noni so she could have the baby."

"And are they…safe?"

Tessa nodded. "Both doing well. It's a girl. Marigold named her Parsley."

"Horrendous."

"I know. Not even poisonous." They had decided that if they were relegated to being flowers, decorative and sweet-smelling, they would be poisonous flowers. Their new names were very carefully chosen.

They exchanged a sigh over poor Parsley, and then Rue rang the bell again: three short rings, pause, one more. The signal for all-clear.

Summer rushed down the hall shouting, "I invited him!" She stopped when they all turned to look at her. "I guess you've figured that out."

Roarke shook his head. Tessa could only imagine what he must be thinking. Especially when Summer reached up to knock smartly on the seventh step of the staircase. There was a pause, the creak of wood, and then the step lifted open, and a woman popped out. Her long, pale hair glowed like moonlight, further underlining her resemblance to a ghost.

"All's well," Tessa told Bryony.

Bryony sighed in relief. Tessa helped her climb out of her hiding spot. It was a priest's hole left over from the dissolution of the monasteries, when King Henry the Eighth wanted to marry a bunch of women and then chop their heads off. They had other places: paneling in the wall that moved to reveal hidden closets, a trapdoor under the heavy rug in the far parlor. A giant barrel in the corner of the kitchen long empty now, save for the occasional spider and women who did not wish to be discovered for various reasons. Most of those reasons involved disgruntled men, to be honest. Earls, a viscount, a vicar.

Holly peeked out from behind a potted tree at the top of the stairs. She was pale, but her eyes glittered like hard diamonds. "It's clear?"

"Clear," Rue called up. She waved her knife, this time in a comforting matter. There was a difference, they had learned. "Come downstairs. I'll make you tea."

Holly wrinkled her nose. She didn't care for tea at the moment. Tomorrow she might crave enough to float a ship into harbor.

"A pot of chocolate, then," Rue amended.

Holly brightened, darting down the staircase. Tessa had no idea where Rue had procured chocolate. Or the cream and sugar it required in the melting pot. They definitely could not afford it.

A countess, however, could afford it.

Along with a man to stay in the gatehouse, with his own bell. And weapons that were not dug out of decades of dust from the waterlogged attic. They had several daggers, three muskets that were older than Tessa, and a pike that may or may not be decorative. They had moved it down to the foyer, where it stood in a basket stuffed with canes and umbrellas. There were daggers slipped between old books piled in a decorative tower next to a vase of flowers. Weeds? Hard to say. Daphne certainly could not.

If Roarke noticed that he stood in a house that was armed to the teeth, he did not say so. Even the chandelier above his head was rigged for easy release onto an unsuspecting intruder's head. The entitled gentlemen they dealt with were rather accustomed to the world falling to its knees around them.

Not in this house.

He did notice something, though. She could see it in his face, in the way he tilted his head very slightly in Rue's direction. Then he said, "Lady Fontes—"

A silence seized the women. Not a soft, gentle hush; this was the moment rain turned to ice and closed around unsuspecting branches and cobblestones. One step and harm could find you from above and from below.

"It's Rue," Tessa corrected him sharply even as Rue lifted her knife again. That knife had poked a great many holes in the list of men tacked to the kitchen wall. Earls, viscounts, weak men with no honor.

Roarke was not weak. Still, he paused. "Rue," he amended. "My mistake."

Rue glanced at Tessa. "Do I need to kill him?"

"Probably not."

Roarke speared her with a glance. "*Probably* not?"

Tessa just shrugged.

"Please don't murder my cousin," Summer said. "He's the only one I like."

"Fine," Rue said, clearly disgruntled. "Dinner is almost ready," she added, before gently bullying Holly toward the kitchens. Bryony had already vanished. She did not care for people at the best of times. She spent most of her time with Foxglove, who adored the attention.

Summer raised her eyebrows. "Well?"

"Well, what?" Tessa muttered.

"Am I toasting the happy nuptials?"

"I told you to stop helping," Roarke said. "Or I'll tell your mother what happened to her favorite diamond brooch."

Summer narrowed her eyes. "You wouldn't."

"I would. And I'd make up a few tales of my own for good measure."

"You—"

"You should go the village," Tessa interrupted them. She needed a moment to think, and she couldn't do that with their friendly, familial bickering. "Fox Hollow has a pub with rooms to let. And stables for your horses."

She had stables, but very little inside them, just enough to care for Foxglove. Also, a few rusty tools left behind. Certainly, no comfortable lodgings for Roarke's coachman. Any lodgings at all, really. He'd have to fight the mice, a colony of cats, and possibly a badger.

"Very well," Roarke said easily, as if he had taken a very ordinary tea in a very ordinary house. "I'll come for you tomorrow," he added quietly, just to her.

A promise.

Possibly a threat.

She couldn't be entirely sure.

DINNER WAS LOUD.

It was always loud. And cheerful. If Tessa was a little more subdued than usual, she did not think anyone noticed. It wasn't just Roarke's offer swirling inside her skull. Iris was leaving.

Tessa was happy for her. Truly.

But she was also a little sad. She was always a little sad to be left behind. Even if that was the entire point of Magpie House. She was building it as a safe wayfaring point. She did not expect any of her guests to stay. They had lives to live, to reclaim, rebuild. Families to return to, when possible. New families, old families. Some had babies; some had inheritances. All of them had secrets.

It had been less than a year, but it continued to astound her the ways Mayfair tried to break down a woman. Follow these arbitrary rules, or else. But only you. And not like that. You bore the responsibility for it all. Oh, some had family members willing to duel at dawn or ruin an earl for mistreating a beloved sister or cousin. But sometimes, families were the problem. Especially when there were fortunes involved.

"Tessa, pass the peas."

She forced a smile and passed Iris the peas. They were her favorite. Iris had been with them since nearly the beginning. She had helped drag all of the rotting tapestries and rugs and the broken tables into the yard for a bonfire. They'd drunk too much wine and howled at the moon. A near-perfect night, to be honest. The first time Tessa had ever spoken in anything above a polite, elegant volume.

She'd loved it.

Tessa had been playing the polite, restrained, ladylike game for so long that she had needed an outlet. Especially as that particular route had not yielded favorable results. Tessa smiled and flattered and danced, and George continued to spend her dowry and steal her annuity.

She eventually managed to steal just enough of the family silver and gold plate to buy a house that was falling down around her ears.

Summer helped. She would have done more if Tessa had let her, including having her live with her in one of her brother's many houses. She had only left for this visit to give the duke and his new bride a bit of privacy.

Tessa had already paid her back the funds lent. Mostly by stealing from the lords and ladies who had put her guests in dire enough straits that they sought her out. Lord Willoughby, who cornered debutantes without powerful families in dark comers, still did not know that it was she who had stolen his diamond-encrusted snuffbox. Lady Tattersby, who had hidden her son's indiscretions, sending brutes after a girl who found herself with child, assumed she had lost her emerald bracelet at Vauxhall Gardens, snagging it on a branch or while dancing.

Tessa, each and every one.

It filled her with what was no doubt wicked joy to do it. It was so rare that justice could be seized. She had not yet managed to seize it for herself, but she would damn sure seize it for others.

For Deirdre.

Never again. Not if she had to steal every snuffbox, brooch, and necklace from here to the Thames. Mayfair would pay its debts.

She reminded herself that Marigold was safe. Iris was happy. And Tessa was baring her teeth at the dinner table. She adjusted her expression again. Ate a forkful of roasted potatoes. Laughed at someone's jest. At least, she hoped it was a jest.

She fought the melancholy. It was self-indulgent. Unhelpful.

She was going to miss her new friend. As her *oldest* friend, Summer knew exactly what she was feeling. And she was a great believer in distraction and misdirection.

"So shall you marry Lord Dartmoor?" she asked.

Loudly.

Roarke was certainly a distraction.

As were the many pairs of eyes suddenly turned her way.

"You'll pay for that," Tessa muttered.

Summer just grinned and popped her chin on her hand, waiting.

"Tessa!" Holly gasped. "You're betrothed?"

"I am not."

"But she could be," Summer said.

"Roarke is right—you are extremely unhelpful."

"Roarke, is it?"

"Stop it."

"Shan't."

Tessa groaned. Glances were being exchanged, whipping past her nose like hail in a storm. "But he did propose?" Iris prodded.

"In a way."

Holly sighed. "Was it terribly romantic?"

Tessa snorted.

"I guess not," Rue said. "Good."

"Good?" Holly echoed. "How can you say so?"

Rue shrugged. "Keeps things tidy, doesn't it? A contract is a contract. No need for flowery promises."

Summer rolled her eyes. "This house needs a poet."

Rue snorted as well. Loudly. "Poets got us into this mess."

"So will you accept?" Iris prodded.

"I don't know," Tessa admitted.

"That's not a no," Summer pointed out.

"It's not a yes, either." Tessa didn't know what to think. And it would not become any clearer with all of the women staring at her. Or with the way Holly sprinkled sugar on a pickle for dessert. Pregnant women really did eat anything.

"What happens to us if you say yes?" Rue asked bluntly.

Bryony pushed her plate away, her cheeks pale.

"Nothing here changes," Tessa rushed to assure them. "I'd make certain of it."

"You could be a countess," Daphne said.

"I suppose so."

The thought of being a countess held no immediate appeal, aside from the help it could provide her friends. The foundations she could build.

Being *Roarke's* countess, on the other hand...

It appealed.

She did not know why. She wasn't sure she *wanted* to know why. It made for a distraction from the melancholy simmering inside her chest. For tonight, let it be enough.

"But to marry the Beast of Dartmoor," Daphne said hesitantly. "Is it safe?"

"Don't call him that."

They finished their meal and drank more wine than was wise. Holly drank pickle juice. Rue refused to let down her guard and drank coffee instead, dark as the mud in the garden. She preferred to be awake and alert for as long as possible. Summer painted more birds over the fireplace in the main drawing room, a silent comfort for Tessa, who collected all manner of birds: larks, swans, swallows.

The moon rose over women laughing too loudly, over spills of wine on the table, the clack of wooden balls and the crash of empty wine bottles in a spontaneous game of bowls in the hall. Bryony set them up in rows, and Summer hung over the banister shouting insults, especially when Tessa's turn came around. "You call that a throw? Stiffen that noodle arm!"

Tessa shot her a grin. "You do know you're not actually supposed to throw it like a cricket ball, don't you?"

"Then where's the fun in that?"

Tessa's grin turned feral. "Shattering the bottles is very cathartic. My walls, however, already have too many holes in them." They'd had to evict some kind of snake from the music room. Something else had chewed through the Tudor paneling in the back hall.

"You're rather violent for someone so short."

"Why do you think I'm so violent?" Not everyone could be as beautiful as Summer, who somehow managed to be lithe and lush all at once.

Summer whistled. "Big talk, Lilliput. Let's see, then."

Bryony blinked, mildly alarmed. Rue patted her arm. "Never mind them—you know they're always like this."

"Delightful, you mean?" Tessa tossed over her shoulder. Her hair had long ago slipped from its pins.

"Is that what that is?"

Summer drained her wine, made a face at the vintage. "Let's go, countess!"

Tessa narrowed one eye, ignoring the very tiny thrill that coursed through her at the title. *No thrill. Bad thrill.* "I could probably hit you from here."

Summer snorted. "You drank as much as I did. You'd have to choose which of the two of me is really me."

"It's a very bad sign that that made sense," Tessa muttered. "Shall we wager?"

"Let's." Summer's eye shone.

Tessa had no money, of course, or certainly none she would waste on the frivolity of a bet, but they never wagered for coins at Magpie House. They wagered for chores. Disgusting ones.

"No chamber pots!" Summer screeched, recognizing the glint in Tessa's eyes.

Tessa relented. Summer was a duke's sister, after all. She wasn't used to chores at all, but had taken to them with a surprisingly small number of complaints. It wasn't as if Tessa was accustomed to chores either before she'd come here. They'd had household servants, a grand house with gold brocade cushions and velvet drapes, and food that magically appeared at the gleaming table in the dining room.

She had eaten bread and cheese and tiny, hard apples for two weeks in a row when she'd first arrived, until her belly rebelled.

At least they had Maggie to deal with the chamber pots now, but she went back home to the village at night and missed most of their truly outrageous behavior. It was a risk to have someone help them at all, but sometimes necessary. It was one of the many reasons the women took on false names. The ones in truly desperate hiding, like Bryony, stayed out of sight whenever help came from Fox Hollow. They followed a strict schedule. They had the bell, Rue. A trick chandelier. Feminine rage.

"Fine." Tessa pretended to grumble mostly because it made Iris laugh. "If I break at least three of the pins, you can wash the bedsheets."

"And if you don't," Summer said, "you scrub the pots after dinner. And you heat all the water for bathing and cart away the old water."

A groan reverberated down the hall, from every woman. Bathwater was the absolute worst. "Done!" Tessa exclaimed. "You don't scare me, Lady Summer." Further wagers were made, and Tessa sent a gimlet eye at each one who bet against her. "Ingrates."

"Less talk! More action!"

"I don't think you should drink wine anymore," Tessa told her friend drily.

"I agree. I much prefer champagne."

"You could try my pickle juice," Holly put in helpfully. "It's much nicer than it sounds."

Summer shuddered.

The others began to chant, like spectators at a pugilism match. Even Bryony joined in, clapping her hands. Tessa lifted the ball and eyed the bottles. There were six of them in total, with other items having been added: a porcelain figurine of a cat climbing a tree, his face oddly flat, clearly made by someone who had never actually seen a cat before, nor heard one described. She was fairly certain it had five legs. He was rather sweet, actually.

"Not Godfrey," Summer said. She leaned down far enough to risk the security of her limbs and flash a generous amount of cleavage, rescued Godfrey the ceramic cat from his terrible fate, and dropped an emu made of shells in its place. "Whoever decorated this house had extremely questionable taste."

The rest of the items consisted of chipped porcelain figurines, cups without handles, souvenirs from trips to the seashore—all gathered from various rooms, and all in dismal shape. The emu was particularly alarming. For something with no discernible eyeballs, it seemed to stare right into Tessa's soul. She aimed for it with a kind of violent glee that was probably unhealthy.

She swung her arm back, ignoring the shouts and the whistles trying to distract her, and made a dramatic show of releasing the ball. It rolled along the wobbly floorboards, sent off course by a protruding nail, returning when it bounced off a broken splinter standing straight up, waiting to snag a hem. It knocked three bottles together, sent one careening into a cup, and toppled a bottle filled with dried flowers dating from the reign of Queen Anne. Not bad.

Especially when the satisfying crack and shatter of glass punctuated the cheers.

"To think you used to dance the cotillion in stuffy old ballrooms for entertainment," Summer said.

The emu's decapitated head rolled toward Tessa. "This is better." She had loved dancing until dawn turned everything pink: the white houses of Mayfair, the marble columns, the cobblestones and carriages. She loved this more.

Iris hugged Tessa hard, eyes misty. "Thank you, Tessa."

"I'll miss you," Tessa said into her shoulder. "But I won't see you off in the morning." She couldn't. People left; she knew that. She didn't have to watch it happen. It just made it worse.

"I know," Iris said.

"Goodbye, Iris."

"It's Lady Winifred now," she corrected Tessa softly. She was finally able to return home now that she had turned twenty-one and the questionable edict in her father's will no longer applied. She could marry whom she liked, when she liked. As an heiress. "Again."

Tessa nodded. Her friend was already gone. "Winifred."

Chapter Eight

When Tessa woke up the next morning, the sun was trying to kill her.

Or perhaps it already had, and she just hadn't realized it yet. It stabbed through the cracked window and right into her left eyeball. She made a strangled sound and tried to sit up. The bedsheets wound around her like chains. She cursed and yanked and huffed. Her head pounded. Her stomach tilted.

She ought to have spent the night thinking over Roarke's proposal, not drinking too much and smashing porcelain animals, however cathartic it was. She definitely should not have started pulling down the wallpaper in the yellow parlor, but there was moss actually growing over it, and she had decided it could not wait a moment longer. She'd managed a section by the door and then went in search of strawberries.

And now, reality.

A lot of it.

Between the state of her body, aching from head to toe, and the smell of spilled wine, reality was a bit of a disappointment.

She wondered what Roarke was doing right now. Was he eating coddled eggs and fried potatoes at the pub? Walking through Fox Hollow regretting his offer? He'd had to carry a pregnant woman through a storm, and then was threatened at knifepoint for his troubles, all within hours of Tessa trying to abduct him. He had surely come to his senses.

But what if he hadn't?

What if the large, silent mountain of a man still wanted to marry her?

Well, not *her* exactly, she had to remind her suddenly very interested pulse. He had chosen her because she was not conventional. Not normal. She wouldn't expect anything of him. He could leave her and never look back.

She forced the knee-jerk twisting in her chest to loosen. This wasn't about her past. She wasn't making decisions for the Tessa she used to be or the Tessa she thought she would be. She had to make a decision for her life as it was right now. For leaky roofs and broken floorboards and women on the run from men with far more power than they would ever have. As the Countess of Dartmoor, she could shield them so much better. They would have food in the larder, sugar and butter, and windows that did not let in the rain and the occasional bird.

Holly and Rue would be safe. Bryony might stop waking up screaming from nightmares. Tessa might never get her dowry back, but at least she had her father's pocket watch. It was gold, inset with enamel flowers, and played a snippet of a song he had hummed under his breath almost every day. It was the first thing she had ever stolen, right from his desk before the solicitors had arrived, her cousin and her dreadful aunt in tow.

I'll gather you roses by the back door, as gold as your hair. One for you, and one for me and one for little lark. Fly away home, fly away home.

She would not need her dowry at any rate, not with two hundred pounds *a month*. Roarke was addled to offer her that much. Or kind. Desperate. She wasn't entirely sure.

Lady Tessa needed the Earl of Dartmoor.

Tessa wanted Roarke.

She wanted the Beast.

She hadn't even realized how much she wanted him, until the possibility presented itself. She could never have imagined he thought of her at all, except to shake his head at her across a ballroom or scowl in her direction when she forgot herself and wandered out into the rain at the end of a particularly energetic ball. He was honest and forthright, and she did not think he would play games with her life. He was too honorable for that, and it made desire curl all the brighter inside her belly. And he tolerated her well enough, if yesterday was any indication.

Could she survive being merely *tolerated*?

Again?

Forever.

She'd once imagined being loved, adored. Having a partner who would encourage her, join in her foolhardy plans. That was a long time ago. Before living out of a trunk, before being shoved aside. Before, before, before.

She could fret and feel sorry for herself, or she could be grateful for an opportunity like this one. Too many women, including all of the ones inside her house at this very moment, never had such options.

It was a lot to think about with a head that felt like it was made of blown glass.

And then her bedroom burst open, slamming into the wall. The sound sent Tessa upright, kicking against the sheets, shouting. The shout made her shout more. Her head fell off and rolled across the floor. She was sure of it. It served her right for beheading an emu. The rest of her followed when the twisted bedclothes abruptly gave way. She landed hard, grunting.

Summer jerked at the shout and shouted back.

It was an awful lot of shouting.

She didn't seem concerned with her oldest friend's decapitation, and too concerned with her own sore head. "I was bringing you tea," she muttered, the tray wobbling in her hands. Her hair was a lopsided bird's nest. "But now I hate you." They stared blearily at each other. "What are you doing down there?"

"Planning your demise."

"How's it going?"

"Hard to say."

"Why is the sun like that?" Summer asked, squinting.

"It hates us."

"I hate it back."

"I can't be a countess," Tessa groaned, climbing rustily to her feet. "Look at me."

Summer rolled her eyes, then clasped her head as if she'd been punched. "Ouch. Possibly you're forgetting the state of the *ton*. I can count on one hand those who don't wake up in worse straits daily."

Fair point, actually.

Summer set the tray down between them, and they drank greedily of the hot, sweet tea, strong as dirt. Perfect. "I might like you after all," Tessa said.

"Shh," Summer replied. Her eyes were closed. "How much wine did I drink?"

"How much wine did we have in the house? Because I think that's how much you drank."

She groaned. "That explains why I feel so dreadful. Holly was singing this morning, and I nearly pushed her down the stairs."

Tessa grinned. "To be fair, she is a horrid singer."

"That poor baby is going to hate every lullaby. Even the ones that aren't about women drowning."

They drank two more cups of tea, ate dry toast, and decided they might not be murdered by the sun after all.

"Let's go to the village," Summer suggested.

"Whyever for?"

"We need the fresh air."

Not fooled for one minute, Tessa waited, eyebrows raised.

"And for your trousseau," Summer added smoothly, eyes twinkling.

Tessa groaned. "I knew it." She scrubbed her face. "I haven't made my decision. And I can't afford a trousseau." What would she even need? Would they have a wedding night? They must, for the marriage to be legal. But then what? It wasn't as if she needed ball gowns or riding habits or diamond brooches. She'd had all of that and sold them off. What she needed now was decent plaster and someone who knew how to deal with a leaky roof.

"Come on." Summer nudged her. "Iris has already left. You don't have to worry about your soft heart seeing her pull away in the carriage."

Tessa swallowed. "Lady Winifred, you mean."

"No, I mean Iris. Your first baby bird has left the nest, and you have a decision to make. You always think better on your feet. And I can't stay cooped up today—between the pickle juice Holly drinks and the bay leaves she insists on burning to protect us from spirits, my stomach simply cannot handle it."

Summer was right. Tessa could stay here feeling sad and nauseated or she could move her body, change her surroundings. Her father had always said: *Move your feet, move your fate.* So, Tessa would go look at bonnets and baby rattles for Parsley.

Move your feet, move your fate.

FOX HOLLOW WAS a village not unlike most villages in England. It was a cluster of stone cottages with a few finer merchant houses, a river, and a bridge where the children threw walnuts. There was a baker and a butcher and even a small dressmaker's shop with an endless supply of ribbon. The pub did a reasonable trade.

As it was early autumn, there were folk in the fields, flowers in window boxes, dogs napping in the shade. Summer and Tessa visited Marigold first, bringing her flowers and pretending that Parsley was a terribly genteel name. Nomi shooed them out before long. They went without protest. Parsley was a tiny, beautiful bundle of high-pitched squeaks and cries that felt exactly like rusty nails inside an aching skull. Nomi clucked her tongue and gave them each a packet of crushed willow bark.

"Bless you," Summer murmured, swallowing it dry. "I am sure that wine was poisoned."

Tessa laughed, then stopped when it rattled her skull. "You're used to vintages that grace a duke's table."

"Are you calling me spoiled?"

"Absolutely."

"Good, I look forward to being spoiled once more." Summer rubbed her tongue. "That is not a normal taste to have in one's mouth. I assure you, good champagne does not linger like this."

"Like old cheese."

"Sweaty feet."

"Sour cabbage."

Summer blanched. Tessa blanched right back. They grinned at each other. But the headache powder and the fresh air helped enormously, and Tessa felt nearly well when they started down the street toward the dressmaker's shop.

Until they saw Mrs. Harris coming toward them, with her tight ringlets and tighter mouth, pursed to disapprove. She wore a day dress that was far too formal and frilly for the warm autumn air and the general mud and dust of a village main street.

Summer groaned. "Not her."

Mrs. Harris noticed them instantly, as evidenced by the straightening of her posture when she saw Summer and the pinch of her mouth when she spotted Tessa.

"I could very easily throw up my accounts on her very shiny shoes," Summer muttered. "Just say the word."

"You're a duke's daughter. She'd probably thank you for it."

Tessa was only a viscount's daughter and far too scandalous for Fox Hollow. For Mrs. Harris specifically, it had to be said. Her brother's wife's cousin had worked at Magpie House for a week and come back with stories about too many ladies and bellies too big for borrowed dresses. They had started hiring family members who could be trusted after that, and making sure the women were hidden away when outside servants had to be brought in. But Mrs. Harris had a long memory and an even longer nose. She had appointed herself the arbiter of good taste and decorum of the village.

"Ladies," she said. She sniffed in Tessa's direction.

Tessa smiled. She always smiled. It drove Mrs. Harris to

distraction, and at any rate, Tessa could not afford to be seen as any more troublesome than she already was. This, at least, she had been trained for. And she needed to keep her credit at the shops. Mrs. Harris knew everyone in the village, and she liked to wield her presumed power like a hammer. She sniffed again.

Summer's expression was one of genteel distaste. Subtly devastating. "That is a most unpleasant sound. Are you ill, Mrs. Harris?" she asked. The cameo around her throat hung on a velvet ribbon, a single bright diamond at its crown. Her dress cost more than Mrs. Harris's entire wardrobe. She might not realize it, but Mrs. Harris certainly did. "Pray, do you have need of a handkerchief?"

Mrs. Harris abruptly stopped scowling suspiciously at Tessa. Her neck flushed. "Oh! No, beg your pardon, Lady Summer." She touched her nose surreptitiously. She glared at Tessa, trying to regain her mantle of composure. "Fox Hollow has a reputation to uphold, you know, Miss Kilkenny."

Tessa sighed. Not another lecture. Even her governess had never been as obsessed with propriety. Honestly, Mrs. Harris expected the king himself to visit Fox Hollow.

"That's Lady Tessa," Summer corrected her, tone steely.

"Of course, of course. But it's only I've heard about Marigold having her baby."

"She did," Tessa replied. "A girl."

"And where's her husband, then? You said he was on his way, and that was months ago. Surely he'll come now."

"I'm afraid he cannot."

"I knew it!" Mrs. Harris crowed, smug and all but shaking with her need to spread the gossip. She motioned to her friend and fellow gossip, Miss Tottenham, who was even now hanging out of her second-floor window, pretending to shake out a rug but clearly trying to hear every word.

"We can't have women like her," Mrs. Harris continued, raising her voice. "It's not proper." She turned to Miss Tottenham, who had all but thrown herself from her house and lunged across the street. Her apron fluttered behind her. "Marigold's gone and had her baby," Mrs. Harris announced. "A *bastard*. As we suspected."

Miss Tottenham's gasp was entirely expected and pure theatrics.

Tessa might have laughed, but they could not afford this kind of scrutiny. Someday a gentleman would come riding through the village searching for a woman who did not want to be found, and Mrs. Harris would send him directly to Magpie House. Tessa would not have it.

"She is not a bastard," she said through her teeth. "She's a *baby*."

"Where's the father, then? Where's this husband?" Mrs. Harris demanded.

"Dead," Tessa said bluntly.

"A likely story."

"His body was only just recovered," Tessa elaborated. She thought of the broken emu, of too much wine, of a safe house where such things were safe. "Without his head. Bloated by the sea. It was quite gruesome."

Mrs. Harris recoiled. "Goodness!"

Tessa was wondering how many grisly details she might conjure up when Summer added, "He was fighting the French." She lowered her voice as if the French might be lurking behind the next fence post. "Terribly heroic. And tragic."

"Oh, I see."

"And now she's all alone, though it was terribly kind of her cousin Tessa to take her in, wouldn't you say?"

"Oh," Mrs. Harris said again.

"Wouldn't you say, Mrs. Harris?" Summer pressed, steel flashing under lace.

"Yes, yes, of course."

"She's with the midwife for a few more days. I'm sure you'd like to bring her a basket. It's the kind thing to do. Especially with the village's *reputation* to consider."

Mrs. Harris's face turned red. Tessa enjoyed the spectacle far more than she should. Mrs. Harris curtsied stiffly, Miss Tottenham curtsied too deeply and wobbled, and then they hurried away, whispering.

"Well done, you."

Summer slipped her arm through Tessa's. "She's going to be a problem."

Tessa sighed. "I know."

They turned to head back home and found themselves across from the pub. Roarke's carriage sat in the courtyard, finer than anything the village had seen in weeks. Possibly months. Some of the children sat in a row on a wall, swinging their feet and shouting out all of the places they would visit in such a carriage. London, India, the moon.

The door opened, and Roarke's silhouette filled the space. Huge, handsome, imposing. He turned his head slightly. He should not have noticed her there, staring like a pewit. But he did, and she was caught, just for a moment. Their eyes clashed. The noise of carts and people buying turnips and flour and horses and dogs washed away. The sun went brighter, the shadows deeper. His gaze found her, held her, if just for that moment.

And then Tessa turned on her heel and fled.

Chapter Nine

REGRETTABLY, COWARDICE HAD consequences.

And it wasn't just having Summer poke fun at her all through the fields and up the drive. Or having to wonder at the warmth in her cheeks and behind her knees. It wasn't a decision hurtling straight for her.

It was finding Rue, Holly, and Daphne standing in the yellow parlor with the half-ripped wallpaper. Bryony was already in hiding, tucked comfortably in some nook or cranny. She never minded the dust or the spiders or the cramped quarters, as long as she was hidden. She never complained. Rue, on the other hand…

"The storm broke another window," she said.

Tessa approached, frowning. "Well, that's hardly unusual."

"But these are."

They moved out of the way to let her in. The glass pane was indeed cracked, but not entirely broken. The latch to lock it was loose. And worse was on the floor in front of it.

Footprints.

Large, slightly muddy footprints.

"None of ours," Rue said, confirming Tessa's instinct. "Too big. We checked."

Trepidation shuddered through Tessa. "Everyone is accounted for?" she asked. Rue nodded. Tessa nodded back. They'd get to the bottom of this, one way or another.

Tessa looked at the footprints again. She would not have noticed them last night. But the mud seemed fresh—surely it would have dried since the storm. She peered outside, into the messy, weedy garden patch along the side of the house. The dirt there was still wet enough to track.

Whoever it was could be in the house right now. Someone sent to drag Holly home. Whoever Bryony was hiding from that she was too afraid to even mention.

"Right," Tessa said when Holly began to shiver. Daphne put an arm around her. "Rue, Daphne, and I will sweep the house, search every room. I'll start in the attic, you two start in the cellars, and we'll meet in the middle. Holly, hide yourself away."

Holly nodded and fled.

"I'll help," Summer said.

Tessa shook her head. "You've helped enough already. I can't ask you to do that."

"Bollocks to that, Tessa Kilkenny."

"You talk to the queen with that mouth?"

"Frequently." Summer reached for a fireplace poker veiled with cobwebs. No one bothered much with the yellow parlor. Mustard-colored walls were not conducive to calm.

"Fine," Tessa said as Rue and Daphne headed upstairs. "Hide yourself just there. The rope for the chandelier is right above you, and you can drop forty pounds of iron and crystal on the head of anyone who goes by."

"I can do more than that. Anyone sneaking about is not likely to use the front hall."

"No, but if they send support, they will. They'll be arrogant enough to march right in through the front door."

"Fair enough."

"But if Wesley comes by to deal with the chicken coop, try not to brain him."

"Fine, fine." Summer wedged herself behind the truly hideous banister.

Tessa grabbed the slightly rusty short sword she kept in the umbrella basket. She wasn't sure if it had once hung above a fireplace or been used to poke at other Englishmen during the Civil War, but it would do well enough for her purposes. It was tempting to find the musket, but loading it and then attempting to shoot relatively straight would waste valuable moments she might need. Worse, an opponent could force it from her. It was better suited to waiting in treetops or on horsebacks for unsuspecting carriages. It was a decent threat, but not much good for follow-through.

She went quietly up the stairs, listening for the sound of intruders. Nothing but the creak of old wood and the wind. The steps to the attic were narrow and steep and tended to groan underfoot. She knew which to avoid and had learned how to listen, how to recognize the oak tree that scraped the window in the side bedroom, the snap of wood when it got too cold. Her heart was loud in her ears, but steady. This was not the first time they had been forced to do a sweep of the house.

The attic was still full of buckets and water dripping. Nothing was overturned, nothing rifled through. But there were dozens of spaces in which to hide. Truthfully, it had kept her up at night more than once. She poked into a chest of moth-eaten linens with her sword. No one jumped out at her. She stabbed at two more chests and into a basket overflowing with what looked to be old curtains. The lopsided armoire with a broken leg and open doors had a story to tell.

A very insulted barn owl erupted from the dark nook, flapping its wings close enough to Tessa's face that her hair moved.

Startled, she shrieked and then nearly stabbed herself with her own sword trying to get away.

So much for stealth.

She was still trying to catch her breath and duck out of the way of the very upset owl when footsteps thundered up the stairs toward her. She whirled, sword up.

Roarke came to an abrupt halt, dodging to the side before she could take off his ear. Or stab him in the eyeball. Gone was the calm, quiet earl. Instead, he looked like an avenging angel, the kind that burned across countrysides. "Are you hurt?"

Tessa shook her head. "Duck!" she squeaked when the owl made another frantic pass between them. One of the buckets fell over, spilling dirty water across his boots.

"What the bloody hell?"

Tessa knew it was the wrong time to laugh. Entirely inappropriate. There was still danger, after all. But the expression on his face was one of fury giving way to bewilderment. She couldn't help it—a giggle snuck free. The way he looked at her only made it worse. She giggled again and then stumbled when the owl took offense. "Oh, settle down. This is my attic, not yours."

Roarke went to the only window, which was, naturally, broken and had swelled shut with the rain. He managed to get it to open through sheer strength of will. And arm muscles. Lovely, thick arm muscles.

Tessa Kilkenny, stop it at once.

Only she had never responded well to scolding, even from herself. And Roarke's arms were still right there. She had the ridiculous urge to bite one.

He used a broken parasol to herd the owl toward the window, and it finally flew out of the opening. Then he turned to rake an eye over her. "All right, devil?"

She'd been called similar, but only since The Incident. And never with such begrudging fondness. She liked it. Too much.

"I'm fine. He just took me by surprise." She frowned. "What are you doing up here?"

"I heard you scream and discovered I could fly. Don't do that again."

She tilted her head. "Your boots are ruined."

"I expect nothing less in this house." He closed the distance between them. "Why are you holding a sword? And why are there women hiding in the walls?"

"Oh. We have an intruder."

He stilled. Something hardened in his eyes. "I beg your pardon?"

"Someone is in the house. Maybe."

"Get behind me," he ordered.

"No need to panic. It's not the first time." Apparently *not* the right thing to say. She'd meant it to be comforting.

His face said otherwise. "Get behind me. And try not to stab me."

"I'm not hiding."

"I never for a moment entertained the idea that you might make it so easy."

She scowled back. "The others are sweeping from the kitchen cellars up. I am sweeping down."

"Alone?"

"It's fine."

"Like hell." He sent her sword a side glance. "On second thought, give me that."

"Like hell," she shot back.

He muttered under his breath, finally unclenching his jaw. "I am twice your size."

She patted his shoulder, trying not to notice how firm and warm he was. How much she just wanted to lean against his back. She knew he'd take the weight of her without blinking. "That's nice for you."

"Do you practice at being infuriating?"

"It's always come naturally."

"That I can believe." He led the way down the narrow staircase, refusing to let her dart ahead. "Why would a housebreaker choose this house? There's nothing to steal." She didn't say anything. He glanced over his shoulder. "Nothing, but not *no one*, is that it?"

She shrugged.

"Tessa, are you in trouble?"

"Not currently." Her cousin wouldn't send someone after her. She had nothing he wanted, nothing at all from her old life except her father's old pocket watch and snatches of a lullaby.

The other women, however, were absolutely in trouble. "You should probably wash your hands of us. Of me."

"Too late."

Why should that send a tiny, hot thrill through her midsection?

Ignoring it, Tessa knocked twice on the floor at the bottom of the stairs with her heel. The double knock sounded back to her, traveling down and back up. "In case they heard me shout. That way, they know not to come running."

"And the housebreaker knows where you are."

"It's not a perfect system," she admitted. "And we only found footsteps. The person who made them is likely long gone." But what had he seen? What did he know?

"Does this happen often?" he demanded.

She shrugged.

"That's not an answer." He swore under his breath. "Or it is, and it's one I don't like. Particularly after Summer nearly dropped a trick chandelier on my head."

"Still time to save yourself."

He only shot her a stern glare as they continued to search bedroom after bedroom: behind dusty drapes, under old beds, inside armoires. They found mouse nests, bits of ribbons, a shoe one hundred years out of fashion, two pennies. No villain twirling his dastardly moustache, waiting to steal one of her friends away. No more footsteps, either.

They met up with the others in the foyer. Summer was already drinking a cup of tea. "All clear."

Rue scowled at Roarke. "What's he doing here?"

"Evicting an owl," Tessa replied. "I think whoever was here has long gone."

"And we don't know what he took or who he saw," Rue said grimly.

"No," Tessa agreed. "We don't."

ROARKE WAS KNOWN to be a calm, unbothered sort of man, if

unlikely to tolerate mutiny.

Tessa was composed entirely of mutiny.

He had never felt less calm than when confronted with the thought of an intruder inside her house. Where she slept. Worse, that she was hunting him with an old sword as calmly as if she were looking for mice in the larder. As if this was a daily occurrence. And considering there was already a plan in motion to deal with such events, it might very well be a daily threat.

No part of him was going to let that stand.

No matter what her answer might be to his proposal.

An answer he meant to get today. Right now.

But he could do without the audience. He'd never cared for one, and like hell was he going to let his cousin meddle any further. She'd gotten him here. It was enough. It was everything, truth be told. But if Tessa said yes, they would have to find their own way. Marriage was difficult enough when you did what everyone expected of you. But this would be different.

Something inside of him rebelled at the thought already, even though he knew it was the right decision. The only decision.

He became aware that the ladies had stopped sending each other meaningful, secret glances in a language he clearly did not speak, and were now instead staring at him. Except for Tessa, who was very pointedly looking everywhere else. She finally heaved a great sigh, mostly because Summer stepped on her foot. Hard. "Oh, very well," she muttered. "Come along, Dartmoor."

She marched into the dilapidated parlor with the painted birds as if confronting an army. Her head was held high, her spine practically a weapon. But he caught a glimpse of her face and could see the vulnerability she has trying to master, to hide away. She was a complicated little whirlwind, this woman. He'd known her to be an angel in Mayfair, but she was definitely a devil at heart.

He found he preferred it.

She started pacing the moment the door closed behind him. He leaned against it, waiting. The light caught her red hair and made it glow. It was as if she carried sunlight inside of her.

"I have questions."

"I am quite sure you do."

She stared at him as if trying to decide if he was mocking her. "You have all of the power."

He frowned. Not quite what he'd expected.

Foolish of him, really. He was the Beast of Dartmoor, after all.

"You're afraid of me," he said bluntly. Disappointment leached through his system. He pushed it back, along with Lara's pale face when she'd met him at the altar.

Tessa frowned back. "I'm not afraid of you," she scoffed.

No one scoffed at him. No one had dared for a long time. "Perhaps you should be." What was he doing? He was meant to be putting her at ease, not warning her off. But he wouldn't be able to stand it if her cheeks paled when she looked at him.

She did not pale. Instead, she rolled her eyes. He could only blink at her for a long moment, a giant of a man who barely fit into fancy frock coats, blinking.

"I'm not afraid that you're going to hurt me."

"Then what?"

"I'm… afraid you're going to steal my house."

He grunted. "I don't want your house, Tessa. It's probably haunted."

She smiled, stopped herself.

"You have my word," he added.

She smiled again, and this time it was apologetic, melancholy, defiant. Angel and devil. Pure Tessa. "That's not good enough, Dartmoor. I am no green girl. I know what a promise means when it is spoken by someone who holds all of the power, all of the time."

"And what does it mean?"

"Nothing at all."

His fist clenched. He was already simmering with outrage on her behalf. "You speak from experience."

She inclined her head, a tiny, fiery queen. "I do."

"We could sign a contract."

Her eyes widened. "You would do that?"

"Certainly."

She looked intrigued, but only for a moment. "But it would never hold up in court. No judge, no solicitor, no bank would recognize it. I would still have no recourse."

He knew he could not convince her that he would never steal her life from her, her ridiculous house, this defiant version of justice she meant to carve out from the world. If things were different, he would love to watch her at her work. To guard her back. She would not believe that either. Why should she? It was as she said—he held all of the cards.

She did not know how she held his attention all of these years. How he sought her out the few times he bothered to attend an event or how he asked after her whenever he saw Summer. Summer had caught on too quickly. But she knew his past, knew the way Lara had felt. She should not have taken it to be her mission to throw them together. Tessa deserved better.

"What if we had Summer witness and sign as well?"

She looked surprised. "Why?"

"The more people you have in your army, the better. Hell, have the duke sign if you like. No judge would go against the Duke of Tremaine. And if we put the house in trust, no one could touch it."

Her lower lip trembled slightly when she exhaled. He found himself desperate to kiss it, to suck it into his mouth.

"I… suppose that could work." He didn't point out that there weren't any options likely to protect her better. He didn't have to. He just waited. Inside he writhed with want and impatience, but he did not let it show. She might not be frightened of his regard for her. But he was. A little bit. It had too many teeth. Too many demands.

She tilted her head. "You're not angry?"

"On the contrary," he replied steadily. "I am furious."

She blinked. "Oh."

"And you're still not afraid of me."

"No."

Such a simple word, and it meant the world. The entire world.

"Shall I tell you why I am angry?"

She nodded.

"Because someone made you feel this way. Someone betrayed your trust." He pushed away from the door. "And I want to know who it was."

She glanced away, glanced back. He advanced on her, not able to stop himself from closing the distance between them. It was too wide, too cold, and soon it would be too real. He would grasp at any beam of sunlight while he could, and he would never, never be the shade that stunted her. "Tell me, Tessa."

She didn't back away, but she did have to tilt her chin up to meet his gaze when the tips of his boots brushed her shoes. He could smell the wind on her, the sun, some kind of wildflower that made him want things he had no business wanting. "No."

He might have growled. He felt it in his chest. "Tessa, I want a name."

She shivered, just slightly, and she did not seem to mind. He narrowed his eyes on her lower lip again. Hungrily.

"Why do you want to know? Are you going to ride out like my knight in shining armor?"

"Someone bloody well should." Didn't she realize that for a man who preferred the quiet and solitude of the moors, this was the most he had spoken in days? That he was not particularly good at it, but that he would also stand in front of the House of Lords this very minute and give a great bloody speech if he thought it would help?

Her smile was tremulous when she was the very opposite. The combination of desire and protectiveness that went through him was enough to stagger him. He had to be careful. So very careful. His head thrummed with warnings and dire predictions and reminders of past failures. Even as his hands reached for her, fingers closing around her upper arms and drawing her closer. Slowly.

Slowly enough to give her ample time to protest. To punch him in the face.

Slowly enough that once she was hauled up against his chest, he was near feral with the need to taste her. Just a nibble. A bite.

Her lips parted. She did not tell him to go to hell.

He was going there anyway.

"Tessa?" he whispered, their mouths barely touching.

"Y-yes?"

"Are you going to let me kiss you?"

What followed was the longest pause of this life. It was excruciating. And he was a man who preferred silence. But not from Tessa. He needed to know what she was feeling, what she was thinking.

She swallowed. "I suppose I should," she said archly despite the catch in her breath and the way her palms curled around his forearms. Pulling him closer, not pushing him away. "For practice?"

He smiled, briefly. Which was a feat, considering he was on fire. "Practice?"

"Well, we'd have to be convincing for the wedding ceremony."

"I can't fault your logic, little devil." He had no logic. Only want and need clawing at him. He paused. His first wife had thought him brutish—too big, too strong, too quiet.

"Roarke?"

"Yes?"

"Have you changed your mind?"

"About marrying you? No."

"About kissing me."

"Hell no."

"Then what's taking so long?" She flashed him a grin. "I have chores to do."

That cheekiness was as captivating as the rest of her, as the twinkle in her eyes, the curve of her hip, the lush suggestion of her breasts under her walking dress. It all burned like kindling the moment his mouth closed over hers. The moment he tasted her, sunshine and fire and mint tea. The very moment she made a tiny sound at the back of her throat, like a sigh.

Let him burn. Let him drown. Only let him have this kiss.

He dug his fingers into her thick hair, angling her head to deepen the kiss, to lick into her mouth until she whimpered. She clutched at him, even as she softened, letting him ease her back into his arms until he held all of her weight. He dragged his lips across her throat, scraping with his teeth, just a bit. He wanted more. Everything. All of her. All of the time.

He pulled back. Her lips were pink now, begging for another touch. Who was he kidding? He was the one close to begging, close to breaking all of the promises he'd made himself all those years ago. Already.

He had never felt peace like this, not unless he was alone on the moors.

He set her back firmly on her feet and took a step back.

"We should probably talk about the wedding night."

Chapter Ten

"THE WEDDING NIGHT?"

She would not blush.

Highwaywomen did not blush at the mere mention of a wedding night.

Highwaywomen of a certain age *definitely* did not blush at the mere mention of a wedding night.

Even with her head still scrambled from that kiss. Lord, the man could kiss. That seemed unfair knowledge to have, as she was not going to be kissing him again. At least not on a regular basis. The way she would a true husband.

But perhaps that was for the best. She couldn't walk around half-addled all of the time.

"I don't recall agreeing to marry you." She had to say it, had to inject a note of levity back into the room before she tried to lick him. A lot.

If you can't be smart, be kind.

How many times had her mother said that? Tessa might not have many memories, but she remembered those words. Her mother even embroidered them on a cushion. Her blasted cousin still had that cushion.

No. She would not think of George. Not now. He would not ruin everything. She wouldn't let him. And so she would be kind. To herself and to Roarke. Because that kiss could undo them. He wasn't overly fond of her as it was. Tolerant, perhaps. And she was not so naïve as to think fondness fueled every kiss. And this one was already too complicated.

She wanted a thousand more.

Even if it hurt a little bit, like nostalgia for something that had never happened.

"You didn't turn me down either," Roarke pointed out, one eyebrow lifting. Back to himself, composed, patient. No longer looking as though he wanted to devour her. He rubbed a hand over his beard.

She straightened her spine. She wasn't for devouring anyway. "I suppose I didn't. But I can't help wondering if you'll regret it. You want to live apart, but don't you need an heir? Someday? You're not getting any younger."

"Steady on."

Her lips quirked at the aggrieved tone.

"There are always heirs to an earldom. Even if they are not sons."

"Oh." She supposed he was right. An uncle could inherit, or a cousin.

"You would prefer children?"

"Not necessarily," she admitted. Frankly, after what little she witnessed of Marigold's labor, she was even less interested.

"There are ways to prevent them."

"For the wedding night."

"For the wedding night."

She licked her lips, trying to forget the kiss, and also trying to fix it in her memory forever. She had assumed marriage was not in the cards for her. And she supposed it still wasn't. Not in that way. "What if you meet someone?" she asked quietly.

He frowned. "I won't."

"You can't be sure."

He nearly smiled. "Tessa, this is the longest conversation I've had all year. And this is the most people I've seen outside of Parliament in easily two years. I'm the Beast of bloody Dartmoor." He stilled, cursed under his breath. "But not you. You could meet someone."

He didn't look particularly pleased at the thought.

"I doubt it," she admitted. "But perhaps."

A muscle in his jaw twitched.

"I suppose we would have discreet affairs," she mused. "Like everyone else in the *ton*." It would hardly be the most shocking part of their arrangement. And since he only wanted to marry her because she was the kind of woman you left behind, she should secure herself any and all options. It was logical. Practical. She should be feeling proud of herself, not whatever this odd sensation in her chest was.

His jaw went hard again, but he only said, "I won't force you. Not ever."

She nodded. "I know." Knowing that made this a possibility. "And a wedding night is just a legality."

He wasn't looking as pleased as she'd assumed he would. He was getting everything he'd asked for, after all. An unconventional wife who would not bother him.

She narrowed her eyes at him. "Whatever happens, this house remains mine."

He nodded. "Agreed. We'll add it to the contract. You can have Rue sign her name to it as well—she's properly terrifying."

She had to smile at that. "True." She tried not to fidget. Was she really going to go through with this? "I don't know what to say."

"Say yes."

Her mouth was suddenly dry. She licked her lips.

"Yes."

Something flared in his eyes, something raw and primal, quickly banked. Then he bowed smartly, back to being the Beast of Dartmoor, roughly the size of a house. "Until tomorrow, then." His voice was a bit lower than usual, gravelly. She liked it. "The archbishop is staying in Bristol, and he owes me a favor. He'll sign the special license. Did you want Summer or the others as witness? Bridal party? Isn't that a thing brides like?"

A bridal party, a wedding breakfast, her friends toasting her with champagne. It would make this feel too real. She did not need to muddle it further. "No, thank you," she replied politely.

Emotions crossed his rugged face again, like storm clouds passing over the sun. She wondered that he had such a reputation for being unreadable when it was all there in his moss-green eyes. They went ever so slightly gray when he was annoyed, and darkened when he was interested. "Very well," he replied evenly. He paused at the door, glancing over his wide shoulder. "Oh, and Tessa?"

"Yes?"

"I would have offered a much higher monthly allowance."

He looked so quietly smug.

"Roarke?"

"Yes?"

"I would have accepted less." She grinned. "You should have bargained harder."

"Tessa, harder is not possible," he muttered drily. "I'd pass out."

Her startled laugh followed him down the hall.

SOMEHOW, BETWEEN MARIGOLD nearly giving birth in a lilac brush during a thunderstorm and a hunt for a house intruder, Tessa had become betrothed.

To the Beast of Dartmoor.

To *Roarke.*

She would be the Countess of Dartmoor. She would finally be able to properly fix the roof. Mrs. Harris could choke on her judgments and her opinions. Tessa would have sugar in the pantry, beef for stew.

And she would have a single night of passion with Roarke.

She could no longer pretend she did not want that, not after the kiss.

And she could bring in more help. Little Parsley could actually go to school one day. And Tessa could buy a pistol that actually functioned. She would still be a highwaywoman, after all. Why should Roarke shoulder the entre financial bill for other men's bad choices?

It was all rather thrilling.

Terrifying.

Summer, naturally, was smug as ten cats. Rue was wary. Holly went through the few books left in the library, mouse-nibbled pages curling with damp, to find her poetry for the ceremony. Everything she suggested contained murder or wailing ghosts.

"You're going to Bristol alone?" Summer asked, disbelievingly. "Surely not."

"Why not? I have my own horse." And Tessa absolutely could not stomach the thought of waking up the morning after the wedding night with Roarke making polite excuses to leave her behind as soon as possible. This was cleaner. More logical. No matter what the look on Summer's face suggested.

She had a horse and a small valise packed with necessities. A few coins, a few items she might sell in Bristol until the monthly allowance was accessible. It might not be very romantic, but it was smart. Safe.

Summer grinned at her. "Are you sure about that?"

"About what? The whole mad affair?"

"No, about riding your horse in the rain for hours."

"I won't melt."

"You certainly won't. Look out the window."

Roarke's carriage waited out front. Tessa's stomach dropped. She had already told him she preferred to ride alone. Was she already to be disregarded, her opinions overridden? Nerves turned to outright trepidation. This was a mistake.

She marched outside, trailing Summer, Rue with her trusty kitchen knife, and Holly with a wedding bouquet of weeds and yellow roses she had tied with a faded ribbon she'd found in a drawer in one of the bedchambers. "Because of that little song you always sing about yellow roses," she had explained. She dropped her voice to a whisper. "They are not very romantic, I'm afraid. In the language of flowers."

Bouquet in hand, Tessa opened her mouth to order away the coachman now opening the carriage door.

Into an empty carriage.

Roarke's family crest might be on the door, but he was not inside. Tessa stumbled to a stop, confused. The coachman bowed. He was not as tall as Roarke, and his arm muscles didn't strain at his shirt, but there was something sharp about him. If he was an ordinary coachman, she'd eat her hat. There was a scar across his throat, as if someone had started cutting and was stopped. He had thick black hair and a kind smile. "My name is Atticus, Lady Tessa. The earl has sent me. This is your carriage now, and I am in your employ. If you'll have me."

Trepidation turned to a tiny, warm flush that she had been seen, if only for a moment. That Roarke took her concerns seriously.

Rue marched forward, which was just as well, since Tessa seemed temporarily frozen to the spot.

"And if she wants you to take her somewhere the earl does not approve of?" Rue demanded. "If someone asks you about her whereabouts? Her companions?"

"The earl instructed me to mind my business."

Rue smiled. It was mostly a flash of very sharp teeth, but it was a start.

Tessa forced her limbs to move. "Thank you, Atticus." She tilted her head. She recalled very well how Roarke reacted to her little housebreaker problem. "And how many weapons are on your person at this very moment?"

"Seventeen."

"Seventeen?" Rue breathed as if he'd just shouted poetry. "He can stay. We are keeping him."

Atticus smiled briefly. He turned to Tessa. "My lady?"

"Well, you're not a puppy, so we aren't just *keeping* you. Are you sure you don't mind? Fox Hollow is hardly London. Diversions are not plentiful."

"I've books for that."

She didn't know what Roarke had told him about Magpie House, nor how much Roarke truly knew about their operation. But it seemed it was enough for him to take care. She'd take that over champagne and cake and flowery wedding announcements in the paper. Any day.

"Very well," Tessa said, and climbed into the carriage.

It probably should not have been so monumental.

It absolutely was.

She tried not to let it loom inside her, and they headed toward Bristol. Women made decisions like this every day, but rarely with such good results. Earls were not generally known for their consideration. Roarke, however, was all consideration. And quiet glowers and wide shoulders.

And extra carriages, apparently.

The walls were lacquered, the cushions dark blue leather. Everything was polished to a shine. Atticus drove the road with care and purpose, keeping the wheels steady. A pity the family crest was upon the door—she could hardly use it to steal from other unsuspecting earls. Never mind; she had Foxglove for that. A wide-brimmed hat and a scarf. And soon, a shiny new pistol.

Anyway, it was probably frowned upon to plan one's criminal activities as you pulled up the lane to the Archbishop of Canterbury's vacation house.

Roarke waited outside for her, striding forward to open the door when the horses pulled to a stop. He pulled the step down, waving Atticus away. And then he smiled at her, that quiet, steady smile, the one that made her toes curl despite herself. The one so few people ever glimpsed. He wore a dark gray coat over a forest-green waistcoat patterned with leaves. His dark hair was swept back as if he'd been walking by the sea. "Lady Tessa."

"Lord Dartmoor."

He offered his hand to help her out of the carriage. His fingers closed around hers, warm and strong. He wasn't wearing gloves. Neither was she. She was forever tearing them.

"Are you ready?" he asked.

She grinned, physically refusing to let her nerves make her morose. If she took herself too seriously in this, she would be doomed. She winked. "Are you?"

He half smiled. "Is anyone truly ready for you, devil?"

TESSA WISHED THE nickname had not echoed in her head in his soft, rough voice, all throughout the simple ceremony. It was not the first time she'd been called something similar—usually having to do with the kind of chaos you wished away. No one had ever said it with such fondness.

It was addictive, that fondness.

Dangerous.

She was not a woman people stayed for, despite fondness. Roarke was proving it to her even now. She had to keep a level head. Stay in the moment. Be grateful and be smart. *And if you can't be smart, be kind.*

Anyway, she was quickly distracted.

Very quickly.

She was married. She was Lady Dartmoor.

And it was her wedding night.

Roarke had rented rooms at the finest inn, The Golden Swan, which was very fine indeed. Everything was swept clean, and there were flowers and beeswax candles on every table and a fire crackling in the old hearth. A mural of a fox hunt raced above the mantel. It was faded, clearly painted at least a hundred years ago. Soot blackened the edges.

"I hope you don't mind an inn," Roarke said, once the door closed behind them and they were finally alone for the first time. As husband and wife. He frowned. "I should have found something better. A country house. Something with dignity."

She grinned. "I happen to have a country house, if you'll recall," she pointed out. "With no dignity to be found anywhere.

This is far better."

"You have a deathtrap with curtains."

"We burned the curtains, actually," she replied cheerfully.

"Dare I ask why?"

"You really don't want to know."

He crossed to the sideboard, where a tray waited, piled high with fruits and pastries. Next to it stood a decanter of wine and one of whiskey. "Drink?"

She rubbed her palms on her skirts, which were patterned with green and white stripes, cheerful but not particularly formal. She'd sold all of her ball gowns. "Whiskey, please."

They drank in silence for a moment as the rain touched the mullioned windows. A cool breeze made the candle flames dance. "Are you cold?" Roarke asked. "I can close the window."

When he moved to do so, she stopped him. "I like them open. It smells like a storm."

She wasn't sure why that pleased him so much, but it did.

They stared at each other a little more, listening to the rain.

"Well, this is all very awkward," she blurted out.

Some of the tension left his shoulders, and he scrubbed a hand over his beard. "I suppose it is."

She tilted her head to the side. "You're the only one of us who's had a wedding night before," she pointed out.

He winced. It was barely perceptible, but she noticed. She filed it away for later. She doubted he would answer her questions about it tonight. Proving her right, he said, "I know this might not the be most romantic arrangement, but perhaps we could not talk about my previous marriage tonight?"

Right. Talk of dead wives was not exactly going to help the awkwardness. She would have bitten her tongue right off if she thought it would help. "I don't need romantic," she finally said, and realized she meant it. "Just honesty."

He smiled then, his rare, bright smile. She wanted to hoard it like gold. "I like that," he said.

She was only going to tie herself in knots if they dragged this out any longer. Marriage equaled wedding night. Without it, the whole thing could be annulled. She'd be just Tessa again.

And she found that her body did not want to wait.

Not one moment more.

She would have liked to say that she approached him slowly, with a sultry come-hither smile. She imagined her hair falling from its pins, a sway to her hips.

Instead, she was fairly certain she launched herself at him.

Chapter Eleven

A LESS STURDY man might have stumbled. Might have staggered and felled them both. Roarke only caught her as if he'd been doing so every day of his life. His arms closed around her, and her toes left the ground. Warmth tingled through her, sparking anticipation.

And then she lost her nerve.

It was a good thing highwaywomen did not have a secret society, or they would kick her out.

Why was crime so much easier than this? Than meeting his moss-green eyes, than knowing he saw her breath catch, saw her lick her lower lip, saw her gaze drop to his mouth? This was an entirely different kind of courage.

She was adept at hiding her own needs. But Roarke wasn't fooled for one second. She knew it on a primal level, in her blood and bones. He saw her. He *noticed.*

And he kissed like the devil himself.

How did such a quiet, steady man, who was known to face down wild horses and shouting politicians with equal and dismissive composure, who did not dance or flirt or even smile overmuch, kiss like *that?* His mouth moved over hers in long, drugging pulls, short nips, a lick of his tongue. His hand was in her hair, pinning her in place. She should have hated it, but she only thought of struggling to see if he would keep her closer. If he would press her more firmly against the wall of his chest. If he wanted her enough to act.

He turned and pinned her to the door, his hand still in her hair. "You'll tell me if you want to stop, and I'll stop."

She nodded mutely. How was she supposed to form words when liquid need coursed through her veins instead of blood? She felt the rasp of his beard at her cheek, the harsh exhales by her ear. Her pulse narrowing to the spot between the legs.

"Say it."

A gentleman's request that made every part of her go hot with need. An order. His forbidding tone was already somehow stroking against her bare skin, and she had yet to divest herself of a single article of clothing.

"If I say stop, you'll stop."

His breath was hot and wild in her ear. "Good girl."

Another kiss, deep and hard, more than enough to steal her breath.

And her pelisse.

He'd unbuttoned it without her even noticing. He pushed the sleeves down, and they tangled at her wrists, keeping her arms back, her breasts forward, pushing against the neckline of her gown. He bent his head to dip his tongue under the edge of the fabric. Shivers followed every bit of skin he touched. His breath was hot and ragged.

His exquisite control wavered for a moment, and he jerked her pelisse free, turning her to face the door. The painted wood was cool on her cheek. He unlaced her dress and pushed it slowly, as if unwrapping a gift. Her short stays followed, and then her chemise. Her breath caught as she felt him at her back, still fully clothed while she wore only her silk stockings and the heat gathering between her thighs.

He smoothed his hand down her bare spine. "Are you a virgin, Tessa?"

She hesitated. She was supposed to say yes. But she was a thirty-one-year-old woman and no more a virgin than he was.

Would it bother him? Society said it should. Not that she could ever compare her few experiences with anything that happened between them.

The air was charged with electricity. The lightning outside the window might well have been created by them every time his tongue found hers, every time she felt the shift of his muscles under his shirt. The flex of his arms. His thick thighs against hers.

"Answer me, Tessa." She'd nearly forgotten what the question was when he caught her chin in his hand, turning her head. "There's no judgment here," he said quietly. "Not between us."

She licked her lips. His eyes flared. She felt something powerful flare in her chest in response.

"I only need to know how best to take care of you," he added.

Such a statement should not have had her eyes stinging with the threat of tears. No one had ever said such a thing to her, under any circumstances. She swallowed to make sure her voice did not wobble and give her away. "I am not."

He grinned, brief and unexpected. "Thank God."

She grinned back with a small, startled laugh. "Does that alter your plans?"

"Only the execution." He pushed into her, pressing his hardness against the seam of her backside. She nearly moaned at the contact. She was trapped, and she had never expected for it to feel so delicious. So freeing.

She did moan when he tugged her earlobe between his teeth, moving his fingers down the side of her rib cage, over her hip. He grazed her quim, just barely. That lightning again. He slid a finger between her folds, then another, teasing. Her breath stuttered.

He bit gently at the spot where her neck met her shoulder, even as he slid deep inside of her. The sensations rocked through her until there was nothing but the slide and friction of his fingers entering her again and again, curling to brush a spot that made her gasp. Pleasure coiled inside of her until he circled her nub with his thumb, and she simply fell apart.

She felt flushed, tingling all over. And he was still wearing every stitch of clothing he'd arrived in. She reached back. "I want to feel you."

"Not yet," he murmured.

"*Roarke.*" She'd never heard that edge of neediness in her own voice before, the command laced with what might be a touch of begging. She might have felt embarrassed, but there was no room for it. Not when he spun her back around, towering over her, surrounding her completely.

"Not until I say so. Not until you're ready."

"I'm ready."

"Little devil, you're nowhere near ready."

Her quim went hot and slick at the promise, the intensity in him.

"I've barely touched you," he continued, ruthlessly patient and soft, even as he knelt in front of her. "You haven't even screamed my name yet."

She blinked down at him, still fuzzy from her climax. If she hadn't screamed his name, it was only because she didn't have the breath to.

His hands closed over her hips. "If this is our only night, I plan to give you a lifetime's worth of orgasms."

His mouth brushed over her most intimate flesh. She nearly came again right then and there. Her body jerked, quite out of her control. "I might not survive that."

"Then I'll give you as many as you can handle. I'll have you come on my tongue screaming, and then I'll have you beg me for more."

She had never considered words to be particularly erotic before.

But then again, she had never heard them whispered at her from a rugged, giant man kneeling between her thighs.

"Roarke."

The low chuckle was definitely something else he'd learned from the devil himself. "Barely a whisper of my name," he murmured. "I know we can do better than that."

He licked at her, flattening his tongue over her bud, stiffening it to circle, finally sucking it right into his mouth like candy. His strong hands parted her, kept her pinned to the door, even as he moved her leg over his shoulder. She was open to him, bared utterly.

And she was coming again.

Just like that. It swept through her, and she made noises she'd never made before.

"Better," he said. "But still not good enough."

"If you want me to scream your name, you'll let me touch you."

He rose to his feet, amused, hungry. "Sit on the bed."

She pouted. She actually pouted.

"Sit on the bed, Tessa."

She crossed the room and sank on the edge of the mattress. He followed her, shrugging out of his waistcoat, loosening his cravat, never once dropping her gaze. How was it possible that she felt as though he was still touching her when he was out of reach? Just with that glance, demanding, patient, aroused, thrilling. He pulled off his shirt, and the expanse of his chest, his warm muscles and thickness, made her swallow. She wanted her mouth on him. On the ridge of muscle, the pelt of hair, the faint scar under his collarbone. His thighs. Everywhere.

He walked toward her, not rushing, but inevitable all the same.

He stepped between her legs, forcing them apart, and kept going, guiding her backward on the bed. She ran her hands over every part of him that she could reach, hot skin over strong muscles. Her thighs fell open; his cock slid over her. He bent his head, sucking at her nipple until she squirmed. She dragged her fingers up the length of him, and he growled into her. "Tessa." There was warning in his voice.

It did things to her.

She kept stroking him until he grabbed her hand, pinning it to the coverlet beside them. She arched against him, taunting him.

Demanding. Begging.

And then he was pushing inside her, inch by inch, so slowly that she nearly started babbling. She lifted her hips to meet him, and he punched forward, filling her. She gasped, stretching around him, greedy for more. He drove into her, again and again, and she rose to meet each thrust. More pleasure swept through her, hitting hard and hot enough to have her back arching off the bed. He followed her, breaths ragged and rough in her ear, swallowing her whole. He pulled out just in time to spend on her thigh.

He bent his forehead to hers, and they stayed that way for a long moment. He finally pushed to his feet and fetched the jug of water and a towel from the washstand. He cleaned her up, softly, while she tried to figure out if she wanted to laugh or cry. She'd never felt like this in her own body. It was as if he had some secret key she'd had no idea was even missing.

He slipped into the bed behind her, curling around her. "Are you counting?" he whispered.

"Counting?"

"Orgasms."

"Oh."

"Well?"

"Three."

"Three?" he scoffed. "That's not nearly good enough."

He pulled her tighter against him, his chest hair tickling her back, one hand around her throat, the other moving lower.

"Keep counting."

Chapter Twelve

"I GO AWAY for a few days, and when I come back, you've gone off to get *married*?"

Tessa arrived home to a deeply disgusted cousin. Marigold looked well, little Parsley sleeping in a basket nearby.

"I've missed you too." Tessa grinned. She had elected to act as though everything was perfectly fine.

Because everything *was* perfectly fine.

Perfectly.

It was perfectly normal to have snuck out of her husband's bed before dawn without a word. To have hurried home so quickly that Atticus had not broken his fast and still had straw in his hair from a night spent in the inn stables. She hadn't run away. She had left expeditiously so as not to make things awkward.

Also known as running away.

But now she was back at Magpie House, and everything would be better. They would hire help, buy furniture that did not shatter under them. And no one had to know that a part of her was still lingering in that bed with Roarke. That she could still feel his mouth on her. Might always.

"Now that is a peculiar expression for a new bride," Rue said, marching across the chipped marble floor. "Are you ill?" She paused. "Are you pregnant? *Already?*"

Tessa rolled her eyes. "I'm not pregnant."

"*Now* who's pregnant?" Summer inquired, coming down the stairs in a stunning and wholly impractical velvet riding habit.

"I have herbs," Marigold said. "I read about them in my anatomy books. I'll make a tea. Just in case."

"And there are French letters," Summer pointed out.

"No one is pregnant," Tessa insisted, but her cousin had already bustled away.

"That's probably for the best," Summer remarked. "We ran out of pickled beets last night, and Holly threw a plate at the wall."

"Goodness."

"She was distraught," Rue said defensively.

"Clearly."

Summer descended the last step and raised her eyebrow. "Well?"

"Well what?" Tessa said.

"Don't be irritating. Are you Lady Dartmoor now?"

"I am."

Summer smiled. "Congratulations. Though I'm still peeved you wouldn't let me be in the ceremony."

Tessa wrinkled her nose and opted to change the subject. "Are you leaving?" Her dress was far too fine for the likes of Magpie House.

"I'm afraid I must," Summer replied. "I've been invited to a house party. I've no doubt it will be terribly dull, but if I don't go, everyone will fawn over Blackpool, and his ego is already insufferable."

"Interesting."

"I assure you, it is not."

"Mm-hmm."

"Married a day and already she thinks she knows everything."

"And now you're being defensive."

"Oh, hush. I'm leaving." She pulled on her gloves. "Try not to stab yourself with that sculpture of the disgruntled faun in the blue parlor. It fell over again and took half the wall with it."

Tessa shut her eyes. "Lovely."

"On the plus side, you can do something about it now."

She opened her eyes again. "True."

Summer hugged her quickly, before Tessa could find an excuse to be somewhere else and not have to watch her leave. But it was easier with Summer. It always had been. Because Summer always came back.

"Thank you," Tessa whispered. "I think."

Summer winked. "It's all going to be grand. Trust me."

"You said that the summer we went to Brighton."

"I did."

"And it was *not* fine."

She shrugged. "But if was fun, wasn't it?" Summer sailed away, laughing. She had already said her goodbyes to the rest of the household, and they had dispersed. Marigold was no doubt reading anatomy texts to Parsley like a lullaby. Rue went up to the attic to rummage, and Tessa decided she did not want to ask what the other woman was looking for. Sometimes it was best not to know. Holly was sitting outside in the sunshine, chatting with her sister. She was pale but happily eating through a jar of pickled radishes with raspberry jam. Shuddering, Tessa went up to her chambers.

She had settled on the peony-pink room, mostly because it was at the top of the stairs, and she liked to think she would hear any intruders before they got past her to the others. It was helpful that Rue did not seem to sleep; she just haunted the halls. Still. All hands on deck.

The bed was unmade. It was always unmade. It was her lasting, tiny act of rebellion. She had grown up in houses teeming with maidservants to make up the beds and feed the fires and take away the tea trays, but most of those servants were also instructed not to pick up after Tessa, not to talk to her, not to let her take one moment of attention from the family. At thirteen she had decided that making her bed as perfectly as possible was the key to not being sent away.

It wasn't.

The habit remained, sharpened into a compulsion of sorts. It made her sweat the first time she left her sheets rumpled and half trailing on the floor. But they were her sheets and her floor and her house, and no one could make her leave. Not ever again.

Still, being a little tidier probably wouldn't hurt her.

And since she felt oddly at loose ends, she wandered about plumping cushions, piling books, untangling ribbons. It was soothing, to ground herself in this room, with its peeling wallpaper printed with peonies, the larks painted along the ceiling line. Three cups stained with old tea that needed to be brought back down to the kitchen.

And her father's pocket watch.

Fly away home, fly, fly away home.

She knew the tune better than she knew her own heartbeat. He had popped the watch open every morning over toasted bread so she could hear the music. He had hummed it to her when she couldn't sleep, and she still hummed it to herself when the nights seemed particularly long. She had been his little lark then. She liked to think he had written the song for her.

It played now, the same snippet over and over again, as she sorted through her thoughts and her belongings. And realized that both were out of order. She knew she hadn't left the basket of stockings that needed mending like that.

Perhaps someone had come in to borrow a book or a claim back the dinner plates from meals long passed and knocked it over. They found the oddest things under all of the beds.

She tucked it back where it belonged and then shut her father's watch and slipped it back inside her green silk dancing slipper. She always kept it hidden in a shoe. No one thought to search them. Not her cousin, nor his mother, nor the butler who was convinced she was stealing. She had been, of course, but only biscuits and old snuffboxes because she thought they were pretty, all enameled and ornate.

She let herself feel hopeful. She projected an air of being

absolutely certain that they could handle anything that came their way, but months of eating hard green apples and burned bread in a house with more holes than walls took a toll. But she could fix all of that now. She could truly see her dreams to fruition.

She would still play the highwaywoman. There were men who needed to pay, by fair means or foul. But in the meantime, she could take a breath.

She could hope.

She could release some of the panic that had begun to nibble at her heels.

But by morning, there were men at the front door.

WHEN TESSA HEARD the hesitant knock, she thought nothing of it. Guests were rare, but the lock was engaged, and probably it was someone with a delivery. They were waiting on a special kind of glue for the decorative ceiling moldings that were falling apart, and deliveries did not always go around to the servants' side entrance, mostly because it was still rather overgrown with brambles. She'd see to it. One day. Eventually.

She peeked through the thick Tudor glass, because she was not an idiot.

A woman stood on the stoop, a basket of what looked like radishes over her arm. It was raining again, and she was soaked through and miserable. Marigold was upstairs with the baby, Rue and Holly were attempting to make something palatable with potatoes and turnips in the kitchen, and Daphne was fighting weeds in the cabbage patch. Bryony was nowhere to be seen, as usual. It had been a couple of days, actually. Tessa would seek her out as soon as she dealt with the poor woman out front. She might need the kind of help they provided.

Tessa unbolted the door, and before she could utter a greeting of any kind, a man shoved the woman aside and nearly knocked Tessa over in his determination to get inside. She didn't have time to stop him. She only had time to ring the bell, once, before two men followed him, considerably larger and rougher looking.

Tessa had no weapon to hand. She knew better. There was no time to curse herself for a fool. Instead, she stood her ground as best she could, glaring with all of the aristocratic displeasure of her ancestors. "What do you think you are doing?"

The first intruder was clearly in charge and clearly just as aristocratic. Blast. She would not be able to intimidate him. It did not help that he was a good foot taller than she was, and much broader with his padded coat shoulders. His cravat was starched into wicked points, his hair artfully tousled. Double blast.

"I'm here for Lady Henrietta Beville."

Henrietta. He was here for Holly.

"You have the wrong house, sir."

"That's not what they said in the village," he said. He reeked of cologne, and it made her nose itch. "They said you've got more women than is proper living up here, and too many in the family way."

Mrs. Harris. Damn the woman.

"My cousin just had her baby, it's true," Tessa said. "But she's a war widow and a vicar's daughter. You've been misinformed." She took a few steps to the left, out of the way of the chandelier, in case someone came along to release it. "There is no Lady Beville here, I assure you."

"I am Lord Beville, and I would advise you not to cross me."

Tessa drew herself up. "And I am Lady Dartmoor," she said sharply. "And this is my house. *Get out.*"

"A countess?" he scoffed. "Living in this heap? Where's your bloody earl, then?"

Oh, how she wished for her dagger. A fireplace poker. A knitting needle.

"See, I don't care if you're married to the king's own cousin. I'm not leaving without my brother's heir."

He was here not just for Holly, but for her baby in particular.

Not encouraging.

The next in line for the earldom, the only one who stood

between Lord Beville and a considerable inheritance. It was not hard to see that he was not here to inquire about her health.

Like hell.

There was a quiet tap behind her.

Tessa took another step to the left.

The chandelier swung down like a battering ram, knocking one of Lord Beville's bruisers arse over tea kettle. He groaned and did not get up.

A victory.

Exceedingly short-lived.

Lord Beville was faster than she would have thought. By the time his bruiser hit the ground, he had already seized Tessa. And placed his knife to her throat.

She froze.

"I'll gut you like a fish," Rue bit out, the rope of the chandelier still in her hand.

"Not before I do her considerable damage," Lord Beville snapped. "I don't want any of you harridans. I only want Henrietta."

"I already told you," Tessa said, trying not to swallow. The blade was already too close. "She's not here. You have the wrong house."

"And I already told *you*, I don't believe you. You're clearly hiding something." He shook his head, and Tessa tensed. She couldn't guess how much control he had over the dagger. "I came just in time. Clearly she is not safe here. So, we're going to search this house, you and I," he said, pressing tighter to her neck. She felt the bite of the blade, the tiny, searing trickle of blood.

His other arm was banded so tight across Tessa's midsection that she could only take shallow breaths. She could only hope that the bruiser had shouted loudly enough when he was hit by the chandelier to alert the others. Surely Holly had had time to hide away.

"You keep your eye on the other one here," Lord Beville ordered his second man.

But Rue was already gone.

Tessa would have smirked if she hadn't been afraid it might result in considerable damage to her throat.

"Goddamn it," Lord Beville said. "Never mind. *Move. Now.*"

"You're making a mistake," Tessa said.

"Shut up." The blade bit again, just a bit. He forced her through the lower-level parlors, sniffing at the state of the house. "You're no countess."

They passed the panel in the wall that hid a secret compartment, the creaking floorboard that led to another priest's hole. The step under which Bryony liked to hide. The house echoed with silence.

And then Parsley gave a fussy cry.

"Who's that, then?" Lord Beville demanded.

"My cousin and her baby," Tessa said as soothingly as she could. But her voice was hard and sharp, despite her best intentions. "But you aren't looking for a babe in arms, are you?"

"We're not," his bruiser said, hulking behind them. "Just for a lady in trouble."

"I'm a lady in trouble," Tessa pointed out drily. "In case you hadn't noticed."

Marigold filled the doorway to her chamber, wielding a heavy iron candelabrum flaking with rust. Gone was the sweet vicar's daughter with no knowledge of the world or her own body. "Get the hell away from my baby. I know six ways to make you bleed out."

"This place is bedlam," Lord Beville muttered, but beyond a glance behind Marigold to look into the room, he did not press forward.

"Lady's not here, guv," the other man said, looking awkward. "It was just village gossip."

Lord Beville swore and forced Tessa back down the stairs. If he had let her go right then and there, she was fairly certain she would have shoved him over the banister.

"Beg pardon, your ladyship," the other man added.

"Oh, shut it, Cole," Lord Beville snapped.

Cole bent to help his partner, who had managed to sit up but was holding his head and groaning. There was blood in his hair.

Lord Beville twisted Tessa's head back to a painful angle. "You'd best not be lying to me."

"You saw for yourself."

He shoved her hard enough that she hit the stone urn on the front stoop, barely catching herself before a proper fall. Lord Beville and his men were already striding away toward their waiting carriage. Tessa watched them go through narrowed eyes.

Lord Beville was going to meet a highwaywoman very soon.

And she was going to be very displeased indeed.

She waited until they had turned off the drive and onto the road before turning back to the house, hand pressed to her throat. Her fingers came away bloody, but not worryingly so. She waited another half an hour before sending the signal that all was clear.

"I want that man's kidneys," Rue announced.

"Agreed," Tessa said. She pressed a little harder on her cut. "This stings like the devil. Lord bloody Beville is going to meet justice on a dark road sometime very soon."

"I look forward to it."

"Beville? Oh, he might have killed you," Holly said, stricken, as she entered through one of the back garden doors. There were leaves in her hair. Daphne had a supportive arm around her waist.

"Where were you, then?" Rue asked.

"I was already outside, so I went up a tree."

A remarkable feat for a woman nearly as round with her baby as she was tall.

"I was not so fortunate," Daphne muttered. "I ended up in the old dovecote."

They winced in commiseration.

"I shall be in the pond if you need me," she added, pulling something best left unexamined from the neckline of her dress. "Just as soon as may be."

"First, I'm going to need more information," Tessa said, calmly but firmly. Holly and Daphne exchanged a glance. Holly's shoulders slumped.

"She's been through a fright," Rue said. "Later."

Tessa shook her head. "Now." She gentled her voice. "It won't change anything," she assured the sisters. "You'll still be safe here. But we *all* need to be safe." She paused. "He would have gone for Parsley if Marigold hadn't turned into an Amazon. I don't know anything about your brother-in-law." She ought to have done better, asked more questions.

Holly bit her lower lip. "You're bleeding."

"She'll be fine," Rue said. "We all will."

"We will," Tessa agreed.

Holly sank onto a bench painted with lambs by someone who clearly hated lambs. "I was married to Lord Beville's brother," she said in a small voice. "As you know."

"Yes, the countess who went missing," Tessa said, searching her memory for the gossip that had run through London. The earl had been found dead at the bottom of a staircase, with a bottle of port. His wife had disappeared—pregnant with an heir who would displace the current Lord Beville, who clearly enjoyed being an earl.

"Her husband was a brute," Daphne added. "With a foul temper not improved by drink. He broke her wrist. Bruised her. And pushed her down that very same staircase, even knowing she was in a delicate way."

"And his brother is worse," Holly said, rubbing a hand over her belly. "Much worse."

"Did you kill him?" Tessa asked. "Your husband?"

"Not me," Holly replied, staring at her feet.

"I did," Daphne announced.

Rue was the first to comment. "Good."

Daphne blinked. "That is not generally the reaction when one confesses to murder."

"I've heard the stories," Rue said. "We all knew to avoid him.

But that didn't solve the problem, did it? *You* did that. And if he refused to observe basic decency, I don't see how he should have been treated any better than he was."

"I don't think the law would agree. Nor God."

"The law will never know," Tessa said.

"And you did not set out to kill him," Holly pointed out. "You only hit him back, and he stumbled."

"But I'm not sorry he's gone."

Rue snorted. "You're human, Daph. Only an angel would forgive him."

"And we're none of us angels," Tessa pointed out. "Devils, every last one of us. And maybe, sometimes, you need a devil to defeat a devil."

Chapter Thirteen

IT WAS NOT three days later that more strangers arrived.

Rue was the first to send up the alarm. She marched upstairs with one of the rusty muskets just as Tessa marched down the same stairs, the second musket at her shoulder. It was a terrible weapon, inaccurate and a pain to load, but perhaps the men out front did not know that.

"All set?" she asked grimly, knocking three times on the stair rail. A knock replied from the priest's hole. Bryony was hidden. Holly whistled from somewhere, and promptly disappeared, as they had practiced several times since Lord Beville's visit. Only Marigold remained in her room, guarding her baby with a fireplace poker.

Tessa opened the door, before it could be opened for her.

She stepped outside, musket at the ready. Three men and a woman in her fifties stared back at her. The men were huge and might well be a problem to contain. But it was the woman, with her steady, sharp gaze, that had Tessa narrowing her own in response. "The house is not open to visitors," she said.

"We can see that," one of the men said, sounding amused. And very Scottish.

"We're sorry for disturbing you—"

"You will be," Rue announced from an upper window, musket trained down upon their heads.

The man looked up even as the others froze. He smiled. "You must be Rue."

"If you know that much, you know I'll shoot you where you stand, pretty boy."

"You think I'm pretty?" He rather was, with long red hair and a quick grin. Idiotic, unfortunately, to be taunting Rue.

"Fergus, enough," the older woman said. Her hair was streaked with gray and curled in a perfect chignon. Her eyes were very black. "We did not mean to take you by surprise, Lady Dartmoor. I am Mrs. Pompadour." A fake name, if Tessa had ever heard one. She liked her immediately.

And no one knew she was Lady Dartmoor yet. To the rest of the world, barring Lord Beville, she was still Lady Tessa Kilkenny. She hadn't sent any notices to the paper. It hadn't occurred to her, to be honest.

She lowered the musket, only slightly. Rue, predictably, only pushed hers further out the window. A piece of glass broke and fell to the ground, somewhat ruining the effect. "I suppose the earl sent you?" Tessa asked.

"He did, my lady."

"A few days late," Rue muttered.

"I'm afraid I'm going to need proof of that." Tessa ruthlessly squashed the urge to ask if he was also on his way. Or if he was even right now sitting inside the carriage waiting on the drive behind them. Of course he wasn't.

"I am glad to hear it," Mrs. Pompadour said approvingly. She pulled a letter from her pocket. It bore the wax seal of the Earl of Dartmoor. Tessa set the musket against the wall despite Rue's sound of disgust coming from above.

The letter was simple, brief. Roarke had sent three men and Mrs. Pompadour to help keep housebreakers at bay, as well as curious owls who had lost their bearings. He had sent her a coachman and a small army. Fergus alone looked as though he could pick up three men at once and toss them across the pond. Useful, that.

If they could keep a secret.

For her, not for Roarke.

"You work for the earl," she said flatly.

Mrs. Pompadour shook her head. "We work for you."

One of the men grinned. "But the earl pays us."

"That's Peter. Fergus you've met. And Lennox."

"I'm Tessa. That's Rue up there."

Fergus winked up at Rue. "Marry me, lass."

Rue snorted and disappeared.

"She will actually shoot you," Tessa felt bound to warn him. He only looked more pleased.

"Peter, you old goat," Atticus called out, coming around from the stables. Tessa noticed the cudgel he held and how he lowered it immediately. He had heard about Lord Beville's visit after the fact, having been in the village at the time. He was still sore about it.

They greeted each other with solid pats on the back, further confirming that Mrs. Pompadour and her men were who they said they were. Tessa let the tension in her shoulders release slightly. Just enough to ease the ache threatening to shoot into her temples.

"I don't think the accommodations will be to your liking," she admitted, telling herself not to feel embarrassed. "You might want to lower your expectations about the house of a countess." Her father's housekeeper would have been horrified. George's mother would say it was no more than she deserved. "I wasn't a countess until a few days ago."

"Nothing a little elbow grease can't sort out, I'm sure," Mrs. Pompadour said. Tessa couldn't place her accent. "Peter, get yourself to the gatehouse and see what needs doing."

"Course, Mrs. P."

Tessa led the others inside, asking them to wait in the front hall. "If you go wandering, you might get hurt."

She undid the first trap. And then knocked on the stair railing again, adding a whistle shrill enough to reach most hidden corners of the house.

Women came scrambling out of walls and stairs and appeared on the stair ladings. Rue scowled, musket lowered but still in hand. Holly suddenly materialized at the end of the hall. Lennox jumped. Bryony, pale as a ghost, emerged last.

"Cor," Fergus said.

"Lovely." Mrs. Pompadour only beamed. "Might I suggest a few more tapestries? No one thinks to look behind them anymore."

Rue looked down at her from the landing thoughtfully. "That could work."

"In my experience, it works every time."

Rue studied her for one long breath. "Would you like to see the kitchens?"

"How sharp are your knives?"

"Sharp as a witch's nose."

"Oh, this is just a delightful house."

ROARKE WENT OUT in the moors, striding over hills and around the remains of stone houses from a thousand years ago. He saw hawks and wild ponies. Heard the wind as it rushed through a circle of old standing stones. All things he craved. All things necessary to his well-being. To his famed equanimity. He came home to quiet halls. Another thing he preferred.

Usually.

The emptiness of the rooms somehow offended him now. The smooth polish of perfect floorboards, the ticking of the clock. He wanted Tessa's perfume of amber and roses. Wanted to hear her cursing as she struggled to fix some broken windowpane or catch a leak before it ruined what remained of the peeling wallpaper.

Didn't just want it.

He needed it. *Craved* it.

It was enough to stagger him.

He'd wanted to be near her for years, and now, after one

night together, he wanted more. It had been a week since she snuck out of his bed before the sun. He was both affronted and amused. He should have expected it. She was, as they'd discussed, unconventional. She would hold to their agreement.

Would he?

The idea of pretending not to notice her for however many more decades was impossible. He wanted to ask her how her day was, what she needed, to bring her wild apples from his ramblings.

He'd never wanted any such thing before.

Correction. He'd always wondered if Tessa would like the moors, but it wasn't until he'd seen her cheerfully wrestling a broken floorboard that he'd thought she'd enjoy the rambling.

Lara, decidedly, had not.

He did not wish to compare his new wife with his first wife, but it was difficult not to. He'd barely known Lara. When he'd come into the earldom at twenty, his marriage followed suit with very little input from either of them. It hadn't occurred to him that she would hate everything about his life and leave for London within days. That his size would scare her. That anything short of polished sophistication was unacceptable to her. Threatening, even. That the country bored her, and boredom did not bring out the best of her character.

At least she had not snuck out of the marriage bed.

He couldn't find it in him to truly be offended. Tessa was honest, and everything that passed between them was both complicated and simple. He wanted her. She wanted him. It was more than most married couples of the *ton* had between them. They might have made it work, in their own way, had things been different.

But it wasn't enough. Not when he remembered how miserable Lara had been in his house, how she had fallen into the arms of several paramours and danced her way through Mayfair, young, beautiful, and rich. She hadn't been happy until she'd left him. Even then, there was an edge to her entertainment. A desperation he never understood.

He wouldn't stifle Tessa. He wouldn't put her in a box and watch her wilt. Not when she was exuberant and brave and cheerful. He had fulfilled the ridiculous promise to his mother, but he wouldn't do it at Tessa's expense.

She had enough money now to make her Magpie House dreams truly bloom. He didn't know exactly what the women who lived with her were hiding from, but he could guess. He knew enough earls and viscounts and marquesses. Mayfair did not dole out enough consequences to such men. His first wife was proof enough. He might not have done a good enough job protecting her, but neither had they. He had never hurt her, but he had not protected her well enough, either. From herself. From a life in the *ton*.

He would protect Tessa. No matter where she lived, no matter where he lived. He'd sent her an army of unusual people who knew which questions not to ask and which secrets to keep to the grave. And they knew how to send housebreakers to the grave. Especially Mrs. Pompadour.

It would have to be enough.

Even though he knew damn well it was not.

Chapter Fourteen

SUMMER'S LETTER CAME very late at night.

Peter stopped the messenger, searched him, and escorted him to the front door while Mrs. Pompadour glared down her nose until he visibly trembled. The letter was accepted and he was muscled off the property, and all before Tessa had made it down the stairs in her wrap.

Rue was sitting on the last step, eating a bowl of blackberries, a knife beside her. Her fingers were stained. "You missed the show."

"What's going on?"

"Someone came to the gatehouse."

Tessa refused to admit the faint hope that Roarke had arrived. He'd made it very clear that her appeal was that she could be left to herself.

She was an idiot.

Tell that to the tiny leap in her ribcage. To the yearning that made her fingers curl into her palm.

Idiot.

"You didn't ring the bell," Tessa said.

Rue shrugged. "I wanted to see if this lot was any good."

"And?"

"Poor sod nearly wet himself." She ate a berry, very loudly. "I'm well satisfied."

Tessa had to grin. "Do you remember when we used to curtsy and make polite chitchat while wearing silk shoes that pinched?"

Rue shuddered.

"I do miss the blackberry scones, though," Tessa admitted, stealing a berry from Rue's bowl.

"I'll get them right one day."

"I know you will."

Mrs. Pompadour came back inside just as Tessa reached for the door handle. The night breeze was cool, scented with smoke from the houses down in the village. Mrs. Pompadour's expression changed instantly from one a general might sport on the battlefield to a woman who offered everyone tea and scolded them about the creases in their hems.

Tessa didn't believe it for a moment.

It was quite the skill, though. She'd have to find a looking glass and practice. She rather relished the thought of being able to make her cousin wet himself with a single glance.

"Everything all right, Mrs. P?"

"Certainly."

"Oi," Lennox called down. "Did you sort it out? The baby doesn't like the fuss."

"Everything is fine."

Lennox spent most of his time walking the halls with little Parsley. She cried blue murder for everyone else, including Marigold. Fergus was a gentle giant who laughed every time Rue threatened him and was incredibly careful around Bryony, the few times she showed her face. Mrs. Pompadour had hired three women to help with the running of the household, although one of them, Paulette, was terrified of her own shadow. She wept and trembled as much as Parsley did.

Mrs. Pompadour handed Tessa a letter sealed with the family crest of the Duke of Tremaine. "For you, my lady."

"Thank you. It's late. You didn't have to get up. I could have seen to it."

"That's what I'm here for."

"Hmm."

"And Peter was getting bored out there. He needed a spot of fun. Tea?"

Tessa skimmed the letter, grinned. "Not tea. Whiskey."

This was exactly what Tessa needed.

A bit of crime.

TESSA HAD BEEN at sixes and sevens since marrying Roarke. Trying not to think of him. Of his mouth on her inner thigh, his hands in her hair. The way he smiled at her, as though surprised he still knew how. It was somehow even more difficult not to think of him now that new floors had been installed all throughout the ground level. One could walk clear to the back of the house without being poked or tripped or otherwise threatened. Rue found it quite boring. Tessa enjoyed being able to focus on something else: the state of the roof, the windows, any number of other lurking disasters just waiting to strike.

Roarke.

Not Roarke, she reminded herself sternly.

Crime.

Which was nearly as thrilling.

Nearly.

But not quite.

She sat atop her horse, tricornered hat low over her head, wearing old-fashioned breeches and a slightly moth-eaten coat. She'd tied a scarf over her nose and mouth. Her pistol was at the ready. It wasn't even raining.

Surely a sign from above.

Summer's letter had told her that Lord Stanhope was leaving the house party where she was a guest and that he meant to take the road not a half-hour from Magpie House.

Lord Stanhope was very, very rich.

Also, an absolute blackguard of a man who deserved to itch in his privates until the day he died. He had many sins to pay for.

And today, Tessa meant to collect.

She had dragged a large branch across the road, just cumbersome enough that the coachman would have to stop the horses to remove it. A rabbit was currently using it as a perch to rest on as he ate a mouthful of greenery. Not precisely the menacing effect she had been hoping for. Still.

The rabbit bounded away a few minutes before Tessa heard the approaching horses. She waited on a small rise, a copse of trees behind her. Should someone give chase, she had several escape routes open to her. And several more traps set out to guard her back. It turned out that the diabolical combination of Rue and Mrs. P was nothing if not creative.

Rue insisted she come along this time, and it lent Tessa a little more confidence. With a shot ringing from the shadows, Rue might appear to be an entire gang. Tessa looked across the road. Rue nodded from her perch in the tree and eased back so she was well hidden.

The carriage approached, painted white with gilded trim. Mud spattered the wheels. Tessa stroked her horse's neck, keeping him still as the others were reined to a halt in the middle of the road. One coachman, one outrider.

Easy as pie.

She waited until the coachman had dismounted and stomped over to the branches, muttering loudly. Tessa guided her horse to the side of the road, pistol aimed at him. He started, spat a curse. He moved, whether to make a run at her or from her, she wasn't sure. He didn't have time for either. Rue's shot rang out, pinging the largest branch by his knee. A lucky accident, to be sure, but she'd take it. He froze. His horses did not. The outrider had to rush for the reins instead of his own weapons.

"My apologies, sir," Tessa said. "But I'm afraid you're going to have to stay right where you are."

He held up his hands. "I'm not risking my life for that toff."

Tessa beamed at him. "Good choice." She hastened to lower her voice, to make it sound threatening. Gravelly. Roarke-like, even. "I mean, good."

She could *feel* Rue rolling her eyes from her treetop.

"Ah-ah." She pointed her pistol at the outrider, who had control of the horses and was now considering his options. "I wouldn't."

"Don't, lad," the coachman said over his shoulder. "Not worth it."

Having everyone acquiesce might not be very dashing or exciting, but it certainly was easier. Still, she stayed in the saddle. She edged closer to the carriage window, angling so she could see Lord Stanhope inside. He was alone. Perfect. He might have a dagger, perhaps even a pistol of his own. Best nip that in the bud.

She shot out his window.

It was very, very satisfying.

He screamed. Shrilly.

Also very satisfying.

"Serves you right, you old lech," Rue shouted. She didn't even try to disguise her voice.

"Stand down, Stanhope," Tessa ordered him. "Or the next bullet finds your spleen."

She was a bit proud of that threat, actually. It was clear, concise. Vivid.

If only she actually knew where one's spleen resided inside the body.

Stanhope made a strangled sound. Tessa moved into view, keeping her pistol at the ready. "Your pouch, sir. Coins, bank notes. That pretty cravat pin."

He sucked in an offended breath. "My grandfather was given this pin by the King of England."

"Excellent. It should fetch a pretty penny, then."

"I'll see you hanged for this."

"Will you? I assure you, I've never heard that before." She whistled once. It was piercing. A command. On the first try. She was rather pleased with herself.

Rue shot at the carriage. Near the carriage. Close enough.

Lord Stanhope turned purple. Oh dear. She hoped he wouldn't faint before handing her his money. She had no wish to rifle through the sweaty man's pockets. "My associate is rather impatient," she said. "And he only gives one warning. Your gold, if you please."

"I'm an earl!"

"You're a blackguard and a lecher, and you prey on young women. You're a widower three times over, each bride younger than the last."

"What are you implying?"

"Be thankful your money is all I'm taking." She reached inside and poked him with the end of her pistol.

He gulped.

"You are boring me, earl."

He shoved a pouch of coins at her, then folded bank notes, and clawed at his cravat pin with shaking fingers. "It's all I have on me."

She dearly wanted to take his carriage and his horses and his clothes and leave him in his smalls in the middle of the road. She would have, were it easier to hide a carriage with an earl's crest on the door. Or to fence it. She eased back before she decided to try it anyway. "Go ahead," she called out to the coachman.

He dragged the branches out of the way and climbed back onto the box. "I don't have any money," he said.

"Even if you did, I wouldn't want it. Walk on."

Tessa waited until the carriage rounded the corner, until the sound of hooves faded, and then waited a little bit longer before pulling down her scarf and grinning into the treetop. "Well done."

"I was aiming for rock. We need better weapons."

"Don't be sour. We have"—Tessa dismounted, peering into the pouch—"enough to feed two more women for several months."

Rue scrambled to the ground. "Enough for a cod's head pie and onions for Holly?"

"Enough for two. Although why?"

Rue shrugged. "She craves them."

"Vile."

"Utterly."

Tessa handed her the pouch. "I'll see you back at the house, then." Rue was already walking away. "Always lovely having a chat, Rue," Tessa muttered.

The sun was warm on her head, the breeze cool on her cheeks. It smelled of mud and burning leaves and the last of the flowers. A good time. She had everything she needed.

Including Roarke.

She turned and started to see him there, leaning against a tree as if he was watching a play on Drury Lane. His voice was rough, amused.

"His spleen, is it?"

Chapter Fifteen

"ROARKE?"

She wasn't entirely sure he wasn't an apparition she had conjured to perfect an already near-perfect moment.

And she refused to examine why he felt like the missing piece.

She was addled, clearly.

But he looked so good, strong, and patient, with wind-tousled hair and that rare half-smile. As if he liked what he saw when he looked at her. She wasn't too small or too much; her hair wasn't too red, her opinions too radical, her nails too chipped.

As if he hadn't just seen her hold up a peer of the realm at gunpoint.

Better, as if he had and he found it… adorable?

She didn't know how to feel about that. About the click of relief and anticipation in her chest on seeing *him*.

"What are you doing here?" she asked. She tried not to squeak, tried to sound nonchalant. Sophisticated. She failed. Of course.

She'd once been so adept at knowing the rules, at following to the letter with a polite smile that showed nothing and a sublime curtsy. But none of that had helped her in the end. It hadn't saved her dowry or made her any more lovable to her family members. She was sure she could pull on the mask again, like a disguise—one so much less fun than a highwaywoman's disguise. But not with Roarke, for some reason. Her polished social skills evaded her.

Probably for the best. If she tried to flatter him, she had the feeling he would just glare at her like she'd insulted his dog. "Clearly I'm not doing anything as interesting as you are."

She smiled. Winced. Mostly winced. "Um."

He raised an eyebrow.

She lowered hers. "You wanted an unconventional wife," she blurted out.

"That I did."

"You have no one but yourself to blame."

"For *your* criminal activities?" he asked drily. "Interesting interpretation of the law. You're right. I should be ashamed."

She winced again. To be fair, in any court in England, *he* could be found culpable, responsible for her actions. Because she was his wife. Because she was a woman.

Anger bit at her.

"I'm only teasing," he said quietly, misreading her expression. She struggled to amend her glower. She'd never glowered when she lived in London. "I'm only glad you didn't steal his carriage, like you did mine."

"Borrowed," she corrected him, wondering why she suddenly felt like smiling. Being around Roarke was exhausting. Exhilarating. Was a person meant to feel so many confusing things all at once?

"Beg your pardon," he said. "*Borrowed*. You're wearing breeches again." He sounded very, very calm. As if he was commenting on the weather. And yet a glance out of the corner of her eye showed his hand curled into a loose fist. His eyes met hers, burned.

She knew exactly how that hand would feel curled around her ankle, stroking her spine. Elsewhere. She swallowed.

She was misinterpreting a flash of an expression. Roarke did not want her, not that way.

Maybe that way. But not in any way that invited permanence.

She was to be easy, forgettable. Disposable.

Tessa's horse, bored with standing about, began to lead them home. She walked beside him, letting him set the pace. Roarke fell into step easily, as if this was all perfectly normal. As if she didn't have a strange sort of pain in her ribcage, like her most vital organs were shifting, dropping.

It was not comfortable.

"Why are you stealing from Stanhope?" he asked.

"Because he's awful." It was the truth, if only part of it. And since he was not linked to any of the women in her house, she was not putting anyone in danger by admitting it was Stanhope, or that he was a donkey's arse. "And convenient."

"Ah." Roarke was not fazed. In fact, he appeared to think that was a very reasonable explanation.

It wasn't. Of course it wasn't. She untied the knot of the scarf around her neck and shoved it into her pocket. It was too warm. She shrugged off her coat as well, as there was no one around to be shocked by her linen shirt.

"What happened to your throat?" There was a growl in his voice.

"Nothing happened to—" She touched her neck, felt the slight ridge of the cut, already healing. "Oh, that."

"Yes," he said with seething, glacial fury, suddenly every inch the Beast of Dartmoor. "That."

"You can't be angry every time you think something has gone wrong," Tessa pointed out, ignoring the warm flutter in her belly. Lower. "You'll spend most of your time very angry indeed. Just this morning, part of the ceiling in the kitchen fell into the soup."

Roarke wasn't listening. His fingers clasped her jaw gently, but firmly. He wasn't going to let her pull away. He tilted her head back, examining the cut. Everything about him screamed brutal vengeance and cold justice, but his touch remained gentle on her skin. She shivered. Just a little. There was something to be said for the contrast.

"It's fine," she said. He was so close that she could smell his soap and the wind on him. "Mrs. P gave me a poultice. It looked like mud, but it did the trick."

"What the hell have Mrs. P and her bloody gang been doing? Making poultices and baking pie?"

"Actually, yes. Peter makes the best raspberry tarts I've ever had."

"Tessa."

"Well, he does."

"Tessa."

She sighed. "It happened before they even arrived. You can't blame them."

The timbre of his voice changed. Darkened. "Who can I blame, then?"

He was still touching her, raking her with his searing gaze.

"Tess, you are trying my patience," he said through his teeth when she did not answer. "And I am much vaunted for my patience."

"I'm sure it's a lovely quality."

He closed his eyes briefly. "You were sent by the devil himself."

"I've heard that before." It had never made her want to smile before, though.

He stroked his thumb near the cut. "Why won't you tell me who did this? I have the powerful urge to separate him from his own skull."

"It's not my secret to tell."

He was outraged. "Someone tried to *cut your throat* and it's not *your* secret?"

Tessa shrugged.

"And why is it a *secret* at all?" Tessa shrugged again. Roarke sighed. "I should have sent an actual army."

They continued to walk side by side in a companionable silence until Tessa broke it. "Why are you here, Roarke?"

"I woke up and you were gone. You ran away from me."

Tessa did not reply. Roarke didn't look at her, but his expression darkened.

"I didn't like it."

Chapter Sixteen

Mrs. Pompadour, with her preternatural abilities, was not surprised to see Roarke, and in fact had just rolled out the tea cart. Paulette shadowed her anxiously. She looked ready to bolt. Or break down in tears.

Tessa narrowed her eyes at the housekeeper. "Did you know he was coming?"

Mrs. Pompadour shook her head. "I did not." She bobbed a quick, efficient curtsy. "My lord."

"Mrs. P," he returned. He didn't say anything else. She didn't seem bothered and so clearly knew him well enough not to be offended. Or cowed. Paulette was another matter. The tremble started in her hands and traveled right up to her mouth.

The others trailed in from all corners of the house. Lennox cradled Parsley in his arms, where she snored with surprising force for a wee thing barely a month old.

"Is that little Parsley?" Roarke asked.

"If you wake her, I will hobble you," Lennox replied. He paused. "My lord."

Roarke only grunted in response. Earls had maimed and killed for less irreverence than that. Paulette squeaked as if she was about to witness a murder.

Mrs. Pompadour clucked her tongue. "We'll have tea," she said. It sounded more like a warning.

She stepped aside, waiting for Tessa to pour. She had not poured tea like a proper viscount's daughter for her guests in years. In fact, she'd been eleven, and it was for a strict, unsmiling governess. And later for George when her aunt was on holiday, and he needed someone to act as a proper lady of the house for his smirking, pretentious friends.

She had not been encouraged to stay and drink the tea.

Still, she didn't know why she felt so nervous. They did not bother with tea etiquette at Magpie House—in fact, had not even had proper tea for the first two months. Rue and Holly did not care who poured; Bryony was scarcely to be seen. But Roarke was here now, sitting like a calm boulder in a spindly chair. Tessa couldn't help sneaking glances at him. At the way the light fell on his strong jaw, the lines at the corner of his green eyes. The way he took up space without even trying. The way he noticed the new, smooth floorboards under his shoes and did not comment but seemed pleased.

Tessa went back to pouring tea. Spilled a little, rolled her eyes at herself. Mrs. Pompadour began to hand them out. Paulette assisted, keeping her eyes down any time she passed Roarke. She tripped and nearly launched a full cup of tea into his lap. He caught it, righted it in her hand. She blanched and started to babble, eyes glistening.

Mrs. Pompadour sighed then waved her away. "Go on and see to the meat pies, Paulette."

Paulette curtsied too deeply and fled.

Rue, Holly, and Daphne sat side by side on a settee with lopsided cushions and eyed Roarke like Tess's old governess might have—stiff-backed, suspicious, sharp. Well, that was Rue. Holly and Daphne tried not to look as nervous as they clearly felt. Marigold wandered in and stole a plate of biscuits. She looked exhausted.

It was not a particularly comfortable tea.

Tessa cast about for a topic of conversation that did not include housebreakers, murderous viscounts, or leaking roofs.

Once upon a time she would have remarked on the fine early autumn weather, the apple harvest, the latest opera, someone's newly acquired horse or brooch or house.

She was clearly out of practice.

Now she just really wanted to know of anyone was willing to help her repair the flue in the chimney in the hideous yellow parlor.

Or if Roarke was really here just because she had left him.

If he thought about their night together as often as she did.

Which was every day.

Every night.

Right now.

Back to tea. Back to polite questions and serene smiles. The closest she could get was to frown at Holly. Holly blinked at the sudden attention. "Have you lost your locket?" Tessa asked.

Holly reached up to touch the silver locket that Tessa had never seen her without. The ribbon around her neck was empty. Holly nodded sadly. "It was in my jewelry box, but the box has gone missing."

Rue tensed.

Fergus popped his head in through the door, incensed. "What do you mean, it's gone missing?"

He and Rue exchanged what could only be described as a murderous glance.

"I think the weasel took it."

"Took my sewing basket too," Daphne muttered.

"And does this weasel have a name?" Roarke asked quietly, but he was looking at Tessa. He clearly thought it was the same man who had attacked her. There was a thunderstorm in his eyes, the kind that came suddenly from the sea and took out everything in its path.

Holly frowned. "I beg your pardon, my lord?"

"The weasel. His name."

"Weasels don't have names."

It was Roarke's turn to look vaguely confused.

"It was an actual weasel," Tessa explained, biting the inside of her cheek because she suddenly wanted to giggle. "We caught him upstairs. He's made a nest somewhere, but we can't find it."

Roarke sat back. "A weasel."

"Maybe a ferret?" Tessa allowed. "A marmot? Are there marmots in England? I can't be sure."

Bewildered, Roarke did not reply.

"Shall I make up your room, my lord?" Mrs. Pompadour asked. "Preferably one without a rodent of any kind?"

The women froze, each to one.

The first test of the Countess of Dartmoor.

Because this was her house. Roarke did not have a room of his own. But everyone would naturally assume the master bedroom belonged to him.

It was currently occupied by one very mean cat and her three kittens. And a cricket no one could catch, but you could hear chirping throughout the house in the dead of night.

They looked at Tessa first, then Roarke. Mrs. Pompadour merely waited. Fergus, joined by Lennox in the doorway, looked to Roarke.

Roarke, bless him, looked to Tessa.

"It's your house," he said simply. "You decide."

She might have married him all over again in the very moment, with no deals to be struck or bargains met. Just because he was Roarke.

She cleared her throat, silently scolding herself for her moment of fancy.

"The Blackbird Room is the only one with any kind of reliable furniture," she said.

"The Blackbird Room it is."

TESSA DID NOT know what to do with herself.

Sleep refused to find her. She paced through her room, picked at a splinter in the window frame, rubbed a spot of paint on the edge of the fireplace. Holly was right. That weasel was a menace.

He'd made off with her left stocking ribbon. She spent an hour searching for it, to no avail. She played the lullaby from her father's pocket watch, but even that didn't work.

Roarke was in the room right next to hers.

She might not know what to do with herself, but she knew perfectly well what she *wanted* to do. With him. To him.

Everything below her neck, from her collarbones to the tickle behind her belly and her thighs, right down to the backs of her knees and ankles, which she had never even considered before, wanted to creep into Roarke's room and then launch herself right at him. Wherever he was—chair, balcony, bed. She wanted to climb him like a magnificent tree. Naked.

Her head, that traitor, was too busy listing all of the reasons why it was a very bad idea.

She was not permanent in any way, thus her appeal. She was too unconventional. Too *much*.

Even if he seemed to like it.

He was probably being polite.

But they *were* married, her hips reminded her brain. It was perfectly proper. Expected, even.

None of the things she wanted to do to him were proper in any way.

Only married on paper anyway, her brain insisted.

Maybe that was enough, her breasts argued.

They missed his mouth. His tongue.

Honestly, he had a lot to answer for. One night, weeks ago, should not befuddle her so. She honestly did not know who would win the battle. Brain, heart, or the hot, anticipatory thrum between her legs.

She did know, in some secret part of herself, that Roarke was somehow the only one who could quiet her racing thoughts. When he was touching her, there was no room for anything else. She'd never known that before. Certainly not with someone else. When she was running through the field or scraping old paint from the ceiling or swimming in the pond until her lungs ached, she felt at home. Quiet within herself.

When Roarke's body moved against hers, nothing was quiet. But everything was quiet.

It was all very bewildering.

Irritating.

Yes, that must be it. She was irritated.

Not at all yearning for a giant of a man who barely spoke to want her as desperately as she wanted him. She had left him, after all. He might be sore about it. He'd even brought it up. She couldn't expect him to come to her room in the hour before dawn. He was probably asleep. Reasonable people were asleep.

She had not slept a wink.

And she wouldn't. She knew that much.

Her feet, suddenly part of her internal battle, took her out into the hall and plunked her in front of Roarke's door. There was a connecting door between their rooms that had long ago stuck shut. Her breath was loud in her ear. She was expecting Mrs. Pompadour, Fergus on his rounds, a weasel. Even if this was her house. Her husband.

Her husband.

It did things to her, that fragment of a sentence.

She knocked softly, probably too softly for him to hear. But if he was asleep and she woke him up, she would simply disintegrate from embarrassment. But if he was awake? If he was thinking of her, even a little? Wasn't it worth the risk?

It wasn't as if her ego was not accustomed to a certain amount of contempt.

She pushed the door open, just barely. Just enough. "Roarke?"

His room was mostly dark, with moonlight flooding through the window to silver the edges of a chair, the bed, the shape of him. The strength of him, the whorl of hair on his bare chest.

Sleeping peacefully.

Not at all desperate for her.

Right, her brain said as she shut the door softly. *That's that.*

The rest of her threatened to riot. She really had become abysmal at following the rules. Even when they were rules she set for herself. She had, at least, proven to herself that sometimes she did not run. Sometimes she opened the door.

Fat lot of good it had done her tonight.

She was mildly horrified to find that she was contemplating a good sulk.

"Ridiculous," she muttered at herself.

The soft whimper of Parsley's unhappy cries approached down the hall, accompanied by heavy footsteps. Lennox. Tessa dove back into her chambers as if she'd been caught pilfering the family silver. She had to laugh at herself. And then she got dressed. If she was going to insist on being awake and looking for trouble, she may as well be productive.

Once the sun had risen, and after a quick breakfast of bread and butter and an apple, Tessa decided to walk the hills into the village to replace her missing ribbon. And perhaps find some fabric suitable for making a stuffed rabbit for Parsley. Normal things.

Not mad things, like poking her head into Roarke's bedroom in the middle of the night.

The long walk with the cool wind pulling at her hair helped, as always. The swallows crossing above her head, the partridge startled out of the long grass, also helped.

Mrs. Harris did not.

It was not exactly unprecedented. And yet, somehow, it always took her by surprise.

Tessa stopped at the bakery first, which smelled like heaven: warm sugar, vanilla, tart raspberries. She bought every currant bun, as they were everyone's favorite, and none of them could make a decent batch for love or money. Luckily, Beth, the baker's daughter, could make them in her sleep. Afterward, Tessa went to the modiste. Madame Colette's considered itself the Little London of the area, with ribbons and silks and bonnets. Tessa passed the bolts of fabric, the printed muslin, the sparkle of silver brooches under glasses, the stacks of *La Belle Assmeblee* magazines. She was only looking for sturdy fabric for Parsley and a packet of hairpins.

Three women waited at the counter, deep in conversation as Madame Colette laid out a new shipment of bonnet ribbons. The talk stuttered into whispers, then silence, as Tessa approached.

She ought to have turned around and walked straight back home that very moment.

But if she wasn't going to let someone like Lord Beville intimidate her, she certainly wasn't going to give the honor to Mrs. Harris. She didn't even have a knife. Only a basket of berry tarts and a sour, smug expression.

Tessa didn't even try to stifle her sigh. "Mrs. Harris," she said. She nodded at the others crowding around like buzzards waiting for the corpse.

Not a good sign.

"With you in a moment," Madame Colette said. She was about as French as haggis, despite her accent. It was customary for modistes to pretend, complete with terrible accents that would make a Parisian street rat weep.

"Thank you, madame," Tessa replied. "Hairpins and something sturdy for a stuffed toy, when you can. Something pretty, though, with flowers."

"I hear you've had a visit from a Lord Beville," Mrs. Harris announced, very much like a town crier. Her ringlets bobbed indignantly.

"Yes, we did."

"Not at all the thing."

"He was looking for someone else," Tessa pointed out. "Someone from the village led him astray. Can't imagine who."

"And another man to your door, *quite* alone, just yesterday," Miss Tottenham added, shocked and thoroughly enjoying every moment of said shock. "And you without a chaperone, Lady Tessa."

"It's Lady Dartmoor now," Tessa replied steadily. *"Countess*

Dartmoor."

It wasn't usually done to introduce yourself so, but needs must. Tessa just wanted to get home to eat currant buns.

There was a pause. Mrs. Harris's eyes narrowed so quickly that Tessa wondered how she didn't give herself a headache. It would serve her right. "A countess?"

"Yes, I was married just recently."

"Nonsense."

Tessa blinked. "I beg your pardon?"

"I would have heard."

"Because we are such good friends, Mrs. Harris?"

The woman sniffed. She would never deign to associate herself with Tessa or Magpie House, and everyone knew it.

But a countess...

"This is another one of your stories," Mrs. Harris insisted. "Spinning your falsehoods. An earl would never take you to wife. You are not *suitable*."

Tessa froze, just for a moment. Barely a moment. But Mrs. Harris noticed—of course she did. She scented a weakness and would not let go.

"I've caught you in a lie, haven't I? Pretending to be a countess and buying supplies for *that baby*. You with more credit than coin."

Tessa was not lying, of course. It wasn't why she paused, however briefly.

You're not suitable.

The last time she had heard those exact words was in her father's house—now George's house. His mother had spoken them with a terse sigh when Tessa snapped at George for changing the sconces in the front hall. She'd been told her mother had chosen them. And her father had been dead all of a week. She'd been nine years old. She was sent to her room, only her room was no longer her room. She was sent instead to a narrow bed no bigger than a cupboard off the nursery. Then she was sent to Aunt Felicity, Great-Uncle Waldorf, and back to her cousin.

Somewhere in between, she had spent a summer with Marigold, until the vicar decided Tessa was not a *suitable* influence. Because they had climbed a tree too high and got themselves stuck. She'd been fourteen.

You're not suitable.

Until she learned to curtsy just so, to pour tea without spilling a drop, to flatter a lord's vanity in French and Italian, to paint watercolors no one cared about, to organize a supper for twelve, to seat everyone in order of precedence, to memorize *Debrett's Peerage*, to smile when she wanted to scream. To be frivolous and entertaining, like a sugar statue.

But she still wasn't *suitable.* It wasn't her manners or her deportment or her lineage. She was simply too much, too odd, too curious. It was just *her*. The essence that made Tessa *Tessa* was wrong.

She'd been reminded of that when Deirdre died in that alley and Tessa learned the true meaning of wrong. The Incident solidified it. She was no longer Lady Tessa but Punch Bowl Ophelia.

She straightened her shoulders. But it was too late. Mrs. Harris had everyone's attention, just as she liked it. It wasn't every day you could wield power over a viscount's daughter as a village merchant's wife.

"Madame Colette, you cannot possibly do business with such a person," Mrs. Harris announced. Loudly. "If you do, we shall leave, and you will lose the patronage of the good, decent women of Fox Hollow and the surrounding villages."

Madame Colette could not afford that. Especially as Tessa and her household rarely had cause to spend their money on ribbons or lace or velvet.

Mrs. Harris's friends tittered. They sounded like hens at the seed trough, pecking, pecking.

Tessa kept her chin high, her expression bland. She would not let them see a reaction and feed on it. This was nothing. This was not a real problem. The roof caving in from rain and taking out the attics and the bedrooms below was a real problem with a very real likelihood of happening. This was just a small woman and her small friends.

Madame Colette forced a smile, apologetic and cornered as a mouse in a cat's house. "I'm sorry, Lady Tessa."

Tessa put the packet of hairpins down on the counter and turned on her heel. She'd use what was left of the curtains in her bedroom, all giant pink peonies instead.

She would *not* punch a woman in the nose.

Not today.

"It's *Lady Dartmoor,*" Mrs. Harris trilled. "Didn't you know?"

Maybe tomorrow.

The door closed behind Tessa on their laughter.

Chapter Seventeen

SHE WAS PERFECTLY fine by the time she reached home.

She produced a basket of currant buns with a dramatic flair. She drank tea. She smiled. She let the cacophony of the house soothe her.

As stated, perfectly fine.

"What's happened?" Roarke demanded.

Tessa blinked up at him from stirring too much sugar too forcefully into her tea. They hadn't been able to afford sugar for months now. "Pardon?"

He scowled. "Your face is funny."

She set down her spoon. *"Pardon?"*

"Not funny," he amended, suddenly hearing himself. He waved a hand. "You're pretty as sunshine; you always have been."

He said it as if it was a thing he had said to her a hundred times before. As if it was a given. "Um."

Rue grinned around a mouthful of currant bun. "Sunshine, is it?" She plucked another bun from the basket and went to stuff it in her pocket for later. Mrs. Pompadour slapped her hand. More astonishingly, Rue let her. "It's for Holly," she grumbled.

"Holly is only eating stewed celery today," Mrs. Pompadour replied.

"With salt," Holly added cheerfully, over her plate of stringy green mush.

"That can't be good for the baby."

"Don't change the subject," Roarke said, his eyes still narrowed on Tessa. "Something's happened."

"Nothing happened."

"You went to the village."

"I often go to the village."

Rue snorted at that. "You do not."

"Traitor," Tessa murmured.

Roarke sat back in his chair, taking up all of the available space at the table. In the room. In the whole bloody house. Did he have to exude such calm strength, such unflappableness? It was perishingly difficult to think when those clear green eyes settled on her as if she was the one taking up all of the space. "Tessa, what happened in the village?"

"Was it Mrs. Harris?" Holly asked, reaching for more salt.

Tessa wrinkled her nose. "No."

"Of course it was," Rue said. "What did that fussy old cow say now?"

"Nothing. Let's have more tea."

"Oh, that bad, was it?" Rue said, and she and Roarke exchanged a glance. "Was she at the bakery?"

Tessa sighed. "No. She was at Madame Colette's. I wanted to find some fabric to make Parsley a toy rabbit."

Marigold's eyes shone. "Oh, Tessa, how kind. She'll love it."

"You said you *wanted* to," Roarke repeated softly. "Which means you *didn't*. Why not?"

She scowled back at him. "Are you a detective now? A Bow Street Runner?"

"Mayhap I should hire one. This house has more secrets than a gaming hell."

Tessa rushed to change the subject. "Madame Colette would not sell to me. It doesn't matter. I can use the curtains in my room."

"Why the hell not?"

"Mrs. Harris did not believe I was countess, and she thinks Parsley is a bastard."

"Parsley *is* a bastard," Marigold said evenly. "But that's not her fault. The blame is on her father."

"Hear, hear," Rue said. "I like this new side of you, Marigold. Perhaps you can teach Paulette not to weep at shadows."

"Not that I would marry him, even were he to ask. Parsley deserves better."

Roarke held up a hand. "What do you mean, she did not believe you were my countess?"

Not *a* countess. *His* countess.

She could not let that thrill her.

Tessa shrugged. "It doesn't matter. Not really."

"She's not the only one who didn't believe you are a countess, either," Holly whispered.

Tessa shook her head sharply. Roarke noticed. He was too keen, saw too much. "Who else?"

"No one." She would not touch her throat.

She didn't have to.

"Goddamn it, whoever tried to cut you didn't believe you either? Would they have reconsidered otherwise?"

"It's fine."

"That tears it." Roarke sighed. It was a soft sound, and the only soft thing about him. His expression was implacable, hard. Cold enough that she might have shivered had she not known him. "We're going to a party."

HE MAY AS well have said he was going to the moon.

There was a very distinct and nearly physical pause, a thrum of silence, and then every single one of them turned to stare at him. Even Fergus, though he had to gallop down the hall to do so.

Roarke folded his arms across his chest, staring back.

"A party?" Tessa echoed.

"Yes."

"You?"

"Yes."

"Roarke?"

"Yes?"

"Did you happen to fall out of the carriage yesterday?" She tilted her head, the minx. "Onto your head? Repeatedly?"

"We eloped," he said, as if she didn't already know. As if the secret of it wasn't eating at him. Did she think he was ashamed? He wasn't. Only cautious. Careful.

Scared to death.

"I did not send notices to the papers," he continued. "Did you?"

"No."

"Well then. That's that."

She shook her head. Rue ate another bun, watching them as though she were at the opera. Holly ate a spoonful of salted butter. Fergus hovered in the doorway until Rue tossed him one of the buns—physically tossed it to him so it sailed over Daphne's head. And this from a lady who used to play the pianoforte for the queen at social events.

It was a problem that this madhouse and its mad inhabitants were growing on him.

"Roarke, you hate parties," Tessa reminded him. "I only ever saw you looming in corners and glowering. Often at me."

He'd only been there to catch a glimpse of her, glowering at anyone who did not make her smile. Who held her too close. He'd cut off his own arm before admitting it. Especially with an audience. "It doesn't signify," he said instead. "I've had an invitation to the Kensington house party. I threw it in the bin."

"Naturally." She said it as though it was endearing, not infuriating, of him.

He could not think of the last time someone had found his silences and reclusiveness endearing. If ever.

"The marquess is a gossip. I went to school with him, and he was the same back then. There will be dozens of people in attendance." He tried to sound as though the thought of it didn't make him want to grit his back teeth. He failed. "Give them two days and the news will have spread to Edinburgh. You won't tell me what is going on here." Though he had his guesses. "But you'll let me arm you."

"With a title."

"You know as well as I do that it will cut as sharp as a blade in certain circumstances."

It was hardly enough. But it was something. He'd see about making sure Fergus and the lads had more pistols as well. And Rue. He'd already ordered one for Tessa. It was simple, nothing flashy that someone might remember spotting in the hand of a highwaywoman. But under the handle, where her fingers curled, there was a tiny bird. She seemed to like birds. He sometimes caught her singing under her breath about a lark flying away home.

"I suppose," she said.

"Your enthusiasm is overwhelming," he noted drily.

She dropped her voice so only he could hear her, despite Rue leaning forward far enough that her sleeve dipped into the jam pot. "You were clear that you did not want a traditional marriage. This seems… very traditional."

"Temporary."

"Ah."

"Needs must."

"I see."

He was botching it. Something moved behind her eyes, something gray and shadowy. He didn't care for it. "It's just a party."

"Very well."

Relief was sharp. When she had come in from the fields, her cheeks were pink from the wind, her hair tangled. She looked good enough to eat.

But her light was dimmed.

She put on a brave face. She clearly excelled at hiding her

disappointment, her hurt. He'd think on that later. For now, it was enough that he could fix this one problem. Someone was treating her ill. And making her doubt herself.

And he would not have that. Not ever.

Men with knives. Debutantes to village gossips. It didn't matter. They would not touch her.

And if he had to parade about in a cravat in a stuffy old house where the men stank of cologne and the women either blanched at his arrival or tried to slip their hands under his coat, so be it. It was a small price to pay.

If he was going to leave her alone, he would have her safe. More than that. She would be *happy*.

God knew he didn't want to leave. He shouldn't have come in the first place. He was breaking his own rules.

Too late now.

Especially when she regarded him with concern bordering on embarrassment. "Are you quite sure?" she asked. "I don't know that the marquess will want the notorious Punch Bowl Ophelia in his house."

"He'll treat you with the respect he treats all of his guests—better, even—or he'll answer to me."

Holly shook her head. "I find that nickname most annoying."

"I suppose I deserve it. It's apt enough," Tessa said.

"Hardly. You did not try to drown *yourself* in a punch bowl, a la Ophelia. You tried to drown a rat."

"*That's* what you object to?"

"Well, it's incorrect. It makes no sense."

"The *ton* rarely does."

"Ophelia would not approve."

Tessa rolled her eyes, but she looked less haunted. Roarke decided to buy Holly her own house. And maybe a horse. Two horses.

He pushed to his feet. Tessa glanced up at him. "Pack your trunk," he said. "We'll leave after luncheon. There's something I have to do first."

Such as visit the village and its judgmental inhabitants—in his shiny, expensive carriage and his best cravat. Like a proper earl. To throw his aristocratic weight around, like a proper jackass. If Tessa wanted to purchase fabric, she would be sold fabric. If she needed bread or glue or silk flowers for the damn bonnet she never wore, she would have them. From the village. Despite this Mrs. Harris.

If Tessa ever truly understood the things he would do for her, he'd be doomed.

SHE WAS DOOMED.

Trust her to be soft for a man who infuriated her to her wit's end.

Roarke had said he wanted nothing to do with her, then he showed up out of nowhere for no particular reason. He sent her an army. He said he wanted an unconventional marriage with no demands, something that had more to do with signing her name in a ledger than anything else, and then he announced they would parade through a house party so their marriage would be public and irrefutable. Just so he could protect her.

Anyone with eyes could see he was the protective sort. No injured bird, stray cat, lost child, or unhappy lady would be excluded from his care. She absolutely could not read into it.

It was not personal. It was not about her specifically.

No matter how warm it made her feel, how desperate to curl into his broad chest. To lick his lower lip. Bite his collarbone. Bite him everywhere.

She was certain ladies did not bite. A governess had surely told her that at some point in her childhood.

Still. She wanted her mouth on him. His mouth on her.

And to think that just hours ago she had felt small. Caged.

He should not have that kind of power over her happiness. Her equilibrium.

Her house.

"Fergus, the fifth step from the bottom is likely to give way at any moment and kill someone. Have it seen to," Roarke ordered, just as the carriage was brought round, already packed with their belongings.

Tessa froze. That was too close to the priest's hole where Bryony liked to hide. "It's already been fixed," she said nonchalantly. Even if she felt very, *very* chalant. Was that even a word?

"Since this morning?" Roarke raised an eyebrow.

"Yes, while you were out."

"Hmm."

She smiled brightly at Fergus. "No need to fuss with the staircase."

He nodded. "Yes, my lady."

Her lungs decided to work again. Roarke studied her for a moment, as if he knew she was lying but could not discern why. She turned the same bright smile on him. "Shall we?"

He nodded, stifling a groan.

"This was your idea," she reminded him cheerfully. She was warming to it. Not because she missed the parties, or the way people had stared at her since The Incident. And not just because Roarke would be with her, and she just felt better when he was. That was something to ignore. With enthusiasm.

But also because there were likely to be many gentlemen there with pasts full of indiscretions.

And purses full of coins.

She would be able to afford a new roof by the end of the week.

"You look positively devilish," Roarke remarked as the horses pulled away from the house.

She sniffed primly. "I'm sure I don't know what you mean."

He raised an eyebrow. She grinned.

But her smile faltered. "I don't wish to embarrass you." Knowing what she did about him and the nature of his first marriage, she imagined he was heartily sick of people whispering about him.

"You won't." He sounded very sure.

"I don't think you realize just how much Society dislikes me."

"I don't think you realize just how much I dislike Society."

There was something comforting about the way he said it. Unflappable.

Still, concern nibbled at her. This was probably a bad idea.

A very bad idea.

She had purposely not put herself in Society since The Incident. She had not been invited since, of course, and she did not push herself into places she was not wanted. Not again. Not anymore.

A thousand small cuts were enough to sever parts of yourself.

But this felt different. She wasn't alone, for one. And it would help her family. Her new family. Still, she found she had to search for her courage, hidden somewhere under self-preservation and bravado. She inched back in the seat at the sudden, crazy urge to fling herself from the moving carriage.

Roarke pinned her with a glance.

"Are you running from me again?" His green eyes gleamed. He saw too much of her. When had that happened? A month ago, he would only notice her to judge her for her antics, like everyone else.

She stilled. "I wasn't running from you before. I was *leaving*," she pointed out. She would not feel like a coward for protecting herself the only way she knew how. "There's a difference."

"Is there?"

"Yes." *Maybe. Definitely. Perhaps not.*

Damn the man.

"Let's see, shall we?" he continued.

She could only watch him, waiting. Anticipation nudged out the worry.

"Come here," he added, voice low.

She felt it everywhere. Heat tingled in her low belly. He didn't move, only stayed sprawled against the seat, slightly too big for the carriage. His boots were planted firmly against the bumps in the road. His coat was folded next to him, and he waited, returning her gaze as he slowly rolled up his shirt sleeves.

It did something to her.

She couldn't say why, only that suddenly she had to bite her lip against a whimper.

Mortifying.

"Tessa," he said. There were threads in his tone: command, amusement, patience. Desire. They wound around her, slipping under her stays, across the top of her spine, along her inner thighs. "You ran from me."

She swallowed.

"So now you'll have to come to me," he continued, as if every word wasn't setting fires inside her body. "I want to remind you of every way our bodies came together. Not because we signed our names in a church ledger; not to join estates or families, or to save your house. Not because of a vow I made a long time ago."

"Why, then?" She had to ask. His words, usually so sparse and direct, were stroking along her skin. She could taste them in her mouth. They were everywhere.

"Because I want to make you feel so good that you lose yourself to it. To me."

She swayed toward him without conscious thought. Wetness gathered at her core, sending bolts of heat down her legs. Her skin prickled, so aware, so sensitive that it was almost painful. In the best possible way.

"But only if you let me," he added. "Only if you choose it."

She licked her bottom lip. His eyes fell to the motion, hungry. His fingers curled against the cushions, as if it was a struggle not to reach for her. It made her feel so powerful, even as she had never felt more vulnerable. "Won't it complicate things?"

"Maybe," he replied. "Let's find out."

"This is a bad idea," she pointed out.

"It's yours to make or unmake."

Damn it, he wasn't going to give in. She had hurt his feelings. She never would have thought it possible. She wanted to make it up to him. Wanted to feel him inside of her again. *Wanted*.

"Maybe complications aren't so bad," she said. She was going to have to reach for him. To prove she wanted this for herself, not simply because of a marriage certificate. Because of rules they had both agreed not to follow. "If we're careful."

She could be logical about this. Sensible. She wasn't a green enough girl to think a man had to love her to want her. Or that she had to love him to want him. They had respect. Rules. Heat.

It was certainly more than most people had.

More than she had ever imagined possible for herself, given her circumstances. And her past. Her present. Everything.

Why not take joy when there was joy offered?

She was absolutely going to break her own heart.

May as well make it worth it.

She reached for him.

It took more courage than she knew she had. A thrill worked through her. It was a heady thing to take your own life into your hands. Not just to help others to do so.

She ended on her knees between his thighs because carriages were not particularly made for grand gestures.

Or perhaps they were.

Chapter Eighteen

ROARKE STAYED WHERE he was, sprawled at his ease against the seat, his hair dark and tousled, his shoulders wide and strong. She could easily picture him as some grizzled medieval warrior just off the battlefield. His eyes were hooded as they tracked her every movement. She might have thought him unaffected. That this was a game to punish her. That he had changed his mind.

Only it wasn't that kind of stillness.

This was the pause before lighting flashed from the sky. That moment you could feel the rain before it fell. Feel the ice before it cracked.

She eased closer, suddenly feeling powerful despite her subservient position. A muscle ticked in his jaw. His thigh twitched under her hand when she laid her palm upon it.

"Well, Roarke?" she asked. Teasing and challenging. "Now what?"

A beat of silence. A flare of those eyes.

And then she was plucked from the ground, weightless, before being deposited on his lap. She had barely a moment to relish the feel of her legs spread on either side of his strong thighs, her heat pressing against his hardness. She was pretty sure a small whimper escaped her, but he was kissing her, digging fingers into her hair and securing her head at an angle that allowed him the best access. The rest of her threatened to go boneless. She was going to turn to smoke, and they were still wearing every stitch of their clothing. How did he always manage to do this to her?

His mouth took hers, hot and hungry and demanding every bit of her attention. The carriage rolled over the uneven road, every bump pushing them closer together, sliding his hardness against her core. Desire throbbed, desperate and dangerous.

He licked into her mouth, dragged his teeth over her throat, sucked on the sensitive spot behind her ear until she could not catch her breath. Who needed to breathe, anyway? She would just die here, a puddle of wants and needs, and be perfectly happy.

When he growled, trying to pull her closer, she made a tiny sound that she had never made before in her entire life. He smiled against her skin. She wondered if she ought to be embarrassed, and then decided she'd rather make him growl again.

He knew it too.

"Devil," he murmured when she writhed against him, pulling at the buttons of his waistcoat.

"*Buttons* are the devil," she said.

He caught her wrist in his hand and brought it to his mouth. "I couldn't agree more." He used his teeth to loosen the button on her short traveling gloves.

"Roarke." Was that her? Panting his name?

A lady did not pant.

As she had already drowned the rules of polite Society in a punch bowl, she was quite happy to pant again. And again. He pulled the offending glove away and set his mouth to her inner wrist. Where apparently a thread of fire lived, connected to her core, to the heat between her legs.

"This is taking entirely too long," she moaned.

"Patience, little devil."

"Roarke—"

"Every single part of you was made to feel pleasure. I intend to prove it to you."

"I think you're trying to kill me." Why wasn't he inside her already? Did he not want her as much as she wanted him?

Was she right back where she started? In a house that was not meant for her? In rooms that did not want her? Doubt was a tiny cut, like a rose thorn. She shifted.

"Where are you going?" Roarke caught her chin and forced her face up to meet his. His tone was patient but implacable. "Whatever put that look on your face stops right now."

She tried to look away. He wouldn't let her.

"Tessa."

"It's nothing."

"You'll tell me this. This is yours to tell. Not one of the secrets of Magpie House."

She exhaled. "I'm afraid." There was something horrible about saying it out loud. Something freeing, too.

Roarke froze. He may as well have turned to stone beneath her. "Of me?" he asked quietly.

"No." She snorted despite the weight of the moment. And the fact that snorting was not generally considered alluring. It was honest, though, and he believed her. And since he had confessed his own fears to her through the tightening of his jaw and the abrupt relief now softening his spine, she could confess hers. "I'm afraid you don't actually want me." She said it too quickly, but she said it. "You don't have to pretend."

"You think I'm pretending?"

"People always pretend." Until they didn't. And it would hurt so much less if they just didn't pretend in the first place.

"Tessa." He said her name like it was cake in his mouth. Sweet, delicate, tempting. Soft.

And then he pressed her palm over the bulge in his trousers. Her gaze flew to his. She couldn't help but squeeze, lightly. He groaned.

The sound soared through her.

His voice was harsh when he spoke again. "Is this pretending, Tessa? I'm so hard for you, have been so hard for you since you stole my bloody carriage, that I am half afraid for my health." He jerked his hips forward a little. "One night was never going to be enough."

She licked her lips. "For someone who does not speak much, you certainly know what to say."

"I prefer showing you."

He pushed her skirts up to her knees, dragging his thumbs up her stockings, over the ribbons, and pressing into her skin. She fumbled for the fall of his breeches and those hateful buttons until he sprang free, smooth and hot and thick. She wrapped her fingers around him, stroking up and down.

"Now who's trying to kill who?" he muttered.

He lifted her breasts free of her short stays and her dress, and the cool air puckered her nipples. He closed his lips around her, sucking a nipple into his hot mouth greedily. She arched, tightening her grip on him. He licked at her slowly, peppered with kisses and pulls, and his voice. That voice. "Are you wet, Tessa?"

She was embarrassingly wet.

Only she remembered she had decided not to be embarrassed. She nodded.

His fingers brushed against her, once, twice, then parted her slick folds. "Is this for me?" Her breath stuttered. He slid a finger inside her, stopped. "I asked you a question, Tessa."

"Y-yes."

His fingers stroked higher, and she clenched around them, moaning. He bent his head to her breasts again, sucking on her nipples with the same rhythm he circled her bud with his thumb.

She came apart with very little warning. A searing heat, a build of pressure, and then she was falling. Her climax pulled at her with the sudden, secret force of an undertow dragging her out. And when she resurfaced, Roarke was laying her against the opposite seat, kneeling as he pushed her legs apart. "One more," he said. "You can give me one more."

He licked up her quim, and quivers and trembles followed

every flick of his tongue. He dragged it through her folds, using two fingers to fill her, pushing in, pulling out, over and over again. His mouth was gentle at her bud, a tiny lick, a soft nuzzle, and when she thought she could not bear another second, something in him snapped. He sucked hard, rolling it without mercy, fingers never faltering. The noises he made were indecent, filthy. Satisfied.

It pushed her over the edge again, and the orgasm rolled through her in sharp, deep waves until her thighs trembled. Roarke turned his head, kissing the quivering muscles before drawing back and sitting down like any earl at a supper party.

Tessa pushed up, feeling mildly drunk. "My turn," she said.

Roarke tucked himself back into his breeches, but he was hard and straining.

She narrowed her eyes. "You're going to let me touch you, Roarke Noble."

"Not yet."

"Why not?"

He wiped his beard with his handkerchief, looking smug.

"Because we're here."

TESSA EMERGED FROM the carriage feeling like a wanton and not minding it one bit.

Roarke followed, every bit as resigned and silent as he usually was. But she knew he was affected now. He shifted. She grinned. His gaze flicked down to her. "Careful, little devil."

She kept grinning. "Why start now?"

She was almost certain he was fighting a smile. And then absolutely certain when he lost. She wanted to keep those rare smiles forever. It fell away when he turned to the castle. He kept them for her, and it made something melt inside her chest. The world got his glowers and his calm, unbreaking stoicism, but he smiled at her. Even in those moments when most people stopped smiling at her. *Especially* then.

He really was the most dangerous person in her life.

And he wasn't even the one who had tried to stab her in the throat.

"Shall we?" Roarke asked drily. "Because you know how much I love a house party."

She giggled.

She actually giggled.

Knives to the throat were safer.

Kensington Castle had been built sometime in the Elizabethan era, and added on afterward by eager inhabitants with very little cohesive taste. Everything rambled—turrets sprang out of nowhere, and marble columns stood next to splintering Tudor beams. It was a mess.

"I love it," Tessa murmured. The mess was comforting.

"You would." Roarke snorted. "There's a doorway that opens to the cellar without any stairs. You could fall to your death. You'll feel right at home."

The front door opened. A cat streaked outside, winding between her ankles. The butler sighed, muttered, then straightened. "I do beg your pardon."

Tessa recalled that the marchioness loved cats. She forced her shoulders to relax. If Lady Kensington did not mind cat hair on the furniture, she could probably put up with Tessa for a few days.

"The Earl and Countess of Dartmoor," Roarke said.

"Welcome, my lord. Your ladyship." The butler bowed, stepping aside to let them in. The foyer floor was set out in a checkerboard pattern, alternating white and black. The walls were the most vivid, an interesting magenta color. Tessa adored it instantly. "The other guests have taken a walk down to the folly, but Lady Kensington is in the library. If you'll wait in the parlor, I will ring for tea."

"I'm here, Forsythe," a lady announced, coming down the hall with a small orange cat wrapped around her shoulders like a shawl. Her black hair shone in the light from the windows, ornamented with diamond pins. There were smile lines around her mouth that came to life when she paused, then laughed heartily. Not at all like a demure marchioness. Tessa's aunt would be horrified. She took it as a good omen. "Why, it's the reclusive Earl of Dartmoor, who refuses merriment of any kind."

"At your service." Roarke bowed, eyes twinkling. "Your collar has teeth."

"Just how I like it. I'm sorry that Kensington is not here to greet you, Roarke. He's hiding."

"Of course he is. Wine cellar?"

"With my new romantic novel, the thief. I'm only halfway through, and he will insist on spoiling it. Oh, but this is a delightful surprise. Kensington said you sent word, but I assumed it was a jest."

"Lady Kensington, I'd like to introduce you to my wife, Lady Tessa Noble, Countess Dartmoor."

Lady Kensington gaped. Tessa smiled uncertainly. "How do you do?"

"When did you develop a flair for drama, Dartmoor?" Lord Kensington boomed as he joined them. He was very tall, and very handsome, with auburn hair that was slightly too long and a scar across his temple. He looked like a marquess as much as Roarke looked like an earl. That was: not at all.

Tessa liked him immediately.

He and Roarke greeted each other the way she imagined brothers would—grins, big handshakes, muttered insults. "Who the hell would marry the Beast of Dartmoor?" Lord Kensington asked.

"The Notorious Punch Bowl Ophelia," Tessa replied. In for a penny, in for a pound.

Lady Kensington's eyes widened. "I *knew* you looked familiar. The Incident."

"Oh, that sounds positively intriguing," her husband said.

Tessa curtsied a greeting and then promptly lost most of her bravado. She shifted from foot to foot. This was a mad plan. She should go home immediately.

Roarke stepped closer, a warm, solid presence at her back. Still uncertain of her welcome, Tessa hesitated. "We can go," she said. "I don't want to cause you trouble."

"Don't be silly," Lady Kensington said, steel suddenly in her soft voice. "This is my house. Anyone who has a problem can sleep in the shed."

"Where she keeps her pet skunk," Lord Kensington pointed out with a smile. He touched her cheek fondly. The cat draped over her protested with a swipe of his claws. "She's my wife, you little ingrate."

The cat proceeded to walk across his shoulder and settle himself inside his very expensive waistcoat, embroidered with gold thread. Lord Kensington scratched his ears. His wife looked like she wanted to kiss him. Thoroughly.

What would it be like to be married in such a way? With such obvious love and affection. Understanding.

As it did not signify, Tessa forced her thoughts back to reality.

"You are entirely too good for him, I am sure," Lord Kensington said to Tessa.

She nearly snorted. Roarke did snort.

"Is this why you declined my invitation to join us for your birthday? Not that I blame you one bit, of course."

"That, and when was the last time I wanted to sit in a circle of aristocrats toasting me on my bloody birthday?" Roarke said.

Lady Kensington nudged her husband with her elbow. "I told you."

"You are resplendent with wisdom and wit, my sweet."

She rolled her eyes. "And you are full of—"

"Lady Kensington!" he interrupted with false scandalized outrage. "You are a marchioness." When she rolled her eyes again, he turned to Roarke. The cat was now thoroughly asleep and purring inside his waistcoat. "Your mother was delightful, Dartmoor, but she did like to stir up trouble." He winked at Tessa, clearly knowing about Roarke's oath to his mother. "I hope you do too."

"Does she ever," Roarke muttered.

"Hey!" She wasn't sure why she was protesting. He wasn't wrong.

"Let's get you settled," Lady Kensington said, rubbing her hands together. "Before the other guests return and ruin the surprise. You have a lady's maid?"

Tessa shook her head. She hadn't needed a lady's maid since The Incident. Never mind the disappearance of her dowry.

Lady Kensington waved that away. "Never mind. I'll send you Francesca. She is brilliant, and it will make everyone else green with jealousy. Puce, even. I can't wait."

Tessa followed her up the grand staircase. The portraits hanging in ornate gilded frames were all of cats. Lady Kensington followed her gaze and shrugged. "Sometimes we have to choose our own family."

Tessa smiled for the first time, a true smile. She thought of a run-down manor house, broken emu statues, splinters in the fingers, women hiding inside the walls. "I think that's lovely."

Lady Kensington smiled back. "Anything you need for the ball tonight, you will let me know. Your presence here will quite make this party the event of the Season. Leave it to Francesca. You shall make an *entrance*."

Tessa could not think of anything she wanted less.

Chapter Nineteen

"THE EARL OF Dartmoor, and the Countess of Dartmoor."

The announcement rang through the exquisitely decorated ballroom. She'd never seen so many candles. They were lovely and smelled of honey, and afforded very few shadows for Tessa to hide in. There were flowers everywhere, in every shade of yellow: roses, chrysanthemums, dahlias. Marble benches carved with more blossoms sat in alcoves created by potted lemon trees. Ropes of ivy crisscrossed from the ceiling, creating the feel of a secret bower instead of a cold, cavernous ballroom. The footmen circling with trays of champagne and wine wore gold masks. It was lavish and luxurious, but also cheerful, just like the Kensingtons themselves.

Once upon a time, Tessa would have loved this. She would have felt excitement instead of apprehension. She would have been welcomed.

She tensed, reminding herself that this was for Magpie House. This was for Holly, whose brother-in-law was trying to murder her. For Marigold, who had been thrown out of the vicarage by a father who preached forgiveness. For Bryony, who would not speak of her past.

For Deirdre.

This was a small thing compared to that.

"Don't you dare run," Roarke muttered, closing his hand

over her fingers on his arm as if he knew she was seconds from pulling away. He wore a dark gray coat and a simple cravat and looked more handsome than anyone else in the room with their perfect pomaded hair and silk waistcoats. "If I have to do this, so do you."

"This was your idea!"

"To protect you."

"You could just buy me a sword."

He smiled at her comment, muttered under her breath.

She was being ungrateful. Cowardly.

And that would not do.

Francesca had spent an hour brushing her hair and plaiting it into a complicated fairy crown, decorated with emerald pins to match her gown. Embroidery trailed along the hem, the neckline, and the edge of her yellow gloves. Francesca had been encouraging, suggesting a carefree smile to combat her nerves. *Do not let them see you,* Francesca said. *Only your shield. They don't deserve the real you.*

Tessa shoved down the anxiety and lifted her chin. Let them choke on Punch Bowl Ophelia. Let them drown. She'd watch with a smile.

"There she is," Roarke murmured appreciatively.

It went straight to her thighs. Which was also distracting.

They stepped forward, into the blazing light of all of those candles.

It started as a ripple, a glance of curiosity, then recognition. Whispers swelled, crashed around them. Tessa could hear "punch bowl," "Tewksbury," "disgrace."

It didn't bother her nearly as much as she had thought it would.

Roarke straightened to his full and considerable height, glaring down his nose at anyone who glanced their way. Threat emanated from him.

It was rather effective.

The whispering guests froze. Wondered if they should move

away.

Tessa only wanted to move closer.

"You're going to make Lord Falsingham cry," she said.

"Good," Roarke replied without an ounce of contrition. "I don't like the way he looked at you."

Tessa softened. "You're going to have to get used to that."

"Like hell."

"You can't make them tolerate me."

"Watch me."

Lord and Lady Kensington joined them immediately, signaling to the entire gathering that they were honored guests. The gossipmongers faltered.

Tessa knew it wouldn't last, but she couldn't deny that she enjoyed it. Just a little. Especially when Lady Dunham recoiled as though she had just bitten into one of the lemon trees. She was the first to ostracize Tessa, to turn her back and sniff, though they had been friends since they were girls. Tessa had turned to poison overnight.

And now she smiled. Because she did not regret it, and the fear she had carried in the back of her mind about this very moment disintegrated. She had Roarke at her side. A house full of friends waiting for her. A purpose. A marchioness who loved cats and her novel-stealing husband greeting her with warm and welcoming smiles.

"Let us be the first to offer our congratulations to the happily wedded couple," Lord Kensington said. Loudly. The man could project. He would not have been out of place on the stage. And he was obviously enjoying the drama. When he clapped, the others had no choice but to clap along.

"Easy, Kensington," Roarke said.

"Not a chance." Lord Kensington bowed over Tessa's hand with a wink. "Lady Dartmoor, would you do me the honor of the first dance?

Opening a ball on the arm of the host who was also a marquess was a badge of acceptance that was fought over. Talked about. Remembered. It wouldn't stop the snide comments, of course. Not all of them. But they would have to whisper. Carefully. Tessa wasn't sure if that was better or worse. She thought she might prefer the brutal truth over candied smiles.

"Kensington," Roarke said, a soft warning.

"Don't fret, old man," Kensington returned. "Dance with my wife. She's pretty enough to distract from your glowering, ugly face."

"Darling, stop teasing him," Lady Kensington said. "You know how he feels about dancing."

Roarke looked at Tessa, then at the crowd gathered like vultures. He cursed under his breath before bowing. "It would be my pleasure, Lady Kensington."

"That was for you," Lord Kensington said in Tessa's ear as he led her onto the floor. "I don't know what you've done to him, but I approve."

"It's not like that."

Lord Kensington cocked an eyebrow at her. "If you say so."

It was a lovely dream, especially here in this glittering place full of diamonds and bared teeth. Sneers that looked like smiles. To have someone stand with her. *Her.* Messy and flawed.

A dangerous dream. She had no business letting it turn her head. She needed her wits about her. *He married you because you are easy to leave behind.*

She promenaded with Lord Kensington, followed the turns and skips of a country dance she barely remembered. The music filled all the spaces between the yellow flowers, and she realized she had missed it. Maybe they could find a proper pianoforte for the house. Maybe Fergus knew how to play the fiddle.

"There," Lord Kensington said. "That wasn't so bad, was it?"

"It was a pleasure, Lord Kensington."

He grinned. "I haven't seen Roarke dance since he was a boy. For that alone, I thank you." He bowed. She curtsied. When the others joined them, Lady Kensington claimed her husband for the next dance.

"I do like him," Tessa said.

Roarke glanced down at her. "Is that right?"

"He puts people at ease."

"He also shrieks when he sees a mouse."

Tessa burst out laughing. Roarke smiled briefly, as if that had been the goal. As if he had been a tiny bit jealous, just enough to make her feel chosen, not trapped.

"Perhaps he was eleven years old at the time," he said grudgingly.

"I'll allow it."

"Did you want to dance again?"

She laughed again. "I might have if you hadn't just sounded like you were offering to chew rusty nails."

He winced. "I apologize." He cleared his throat. "Lady Dartmoor, will you dance?"

She squeezed his arm affectionately. "No, thank you."

"I am fairly certain you love to dance."

"I do." She shrugged. "But you don't, and I don't remember all of the steps to this reel anyway."

He placed his warm palm over her knuckles, keeping her hand in place for a longer moment. "You're a terrible liar."

"I'm a wonderful liar!"

"For a highwaywoman," he whispered, "I expected better."

They grinned at each other, and she could almost forget where they were.

"How about some champagne, then?" he asked.

She made sure her voice was just slightly louder than necessary. "I'd much prefer punch, my lord."

His bark of laughter took her by surprise. It took him by surprise too, if his expression was anything to go by. In fact, it took every guest within hearing distance by surprise.

She'd never felt more powerful. Or smugger, truth be told.

Across the sea of diamond hairpins and pomaded curls, Lord Kensington caught her eye and winked. "Winking at another man's wife," Roarke grumbled, heading toward the refreshment tables.

Tessa tucked herself under a lemon tree and inhaled the sharp citrus scent, feeling better than she would have ever thought in this moment. Disdainful glances were being thrown her way, mouths moving behind painted fans, a sneer here, a scornful smirk there. But she made Roarke laugh. In public. Where she had only every seen him with the unwavering, uninterested stoicism of a stone.

The entire *ton* could drown in the punch bowl.

Or, at the very least, her cousin George.

She ought to have known better than to get cocky. Even inside her own head. Her family sensed that kind of thing, sniffed out any whiff of confidence and descended like pigs on truffles.

"Tessa, don't slouch. It's not ladylike."

Tessa stifled a groan at her aunt's words, shooting like bullets toward her. She did not, however, straighten her already straight spine.

Point for Tessa.

"Hello, Aunt Celeste."

Celeste sniffed. She was a beautiful woman, with the aristocratic bearing of a person who knew they were descended from a line that dated back to before the Battle of Hastings. She wore a soft blue gown with cream lace, and more pearls and opals than a jeweler's shop sold in a year. Her silk slippers must be pinching her toes, given the unhappy purse of her lips. Tessa nearly said so.

"Cousin," George greeted her, sounding bored. But his eyes were sharp. They always had been. He was handsome enough, and it got him out of consequence after consequence. It was no surprise that he was good friends with Lord Tewksbury.

"George."

"Lord Raleigh," her aunt corrected.

"Then he may address me as Lady Dartmoor."

Celeste sucked in an outraged breath. He no longer outranked her. In fact, she outranked her aunt. A small, petty part of her rejoiced at that, if only because they would have great difficulty in adjusting to that fact.

Fine. Not a very small part of her.

Aunt Celeste was turning a very unflattering shade of vermilion. "Everything is a caper to you, isn't it? A lark."

"Mother, don't trouble yourself," George said. "You know she was always ungrateful and rude."

Tessa had been no such thing. But the familiar accusation did deflate her slightly. And he knew it. Damn him.

George shook his head, feigning concern. "I was certain the rumors were wrong. What have you gotten yourself into now? You aren't suitable as a countess, cousin. You haven't the disposition."

He was right about that last part. Countesses probably did not stuff lemons up a viscount's nostril during a ball. She still gave it serious consideration.

Very serious.

His very presence brought back memories of packing her favorite dresses after her father died and George and her aunt took possession of the house. Her favorite books, which her aunt made her return because they now belonged to her son. Even though he had no intention of reading them. The way her aunt was never satisfied with Tessa's posture or smile or needlework. Her French was not good enough; she galloped instead of danced. She was ungrateful, greedy.

Tessa called up the little snippet of song from her father's pocket watch, letting it soothe her, as it always did. She wasn't a young girl anymore. She wasn't even the woman they had helped kick out of Society, older and with very few options. She was a highwaywoman. A countess. And she was humming under her breath.

George sent her a sharp look. She snapped her teeth together even as she contemplated singing at the top of her lungs. Instead, she turned on her heel and left.

She could leave now. *Fly away, fly away, fly away home.* She had the power to make the choice instead of having it made for her. She did not need George or her aunt. Pride carried her to the balcony doors and down the steps into the shadows at the edge of the garden before the all-too-familiar itch to run away tingled in her feet. In her throat, burning with emotions she did not like. Did not want to feel again.

Did not deserve.

But it was there under her skin, and she did not know how to rid herself of it without running. She had improved. She did not need to flee the county or the city. Just the ballroom. Just for now. The dark gardens called, and the shadowy maze under the moon.

No one would notice.

Someone noticed.

"Are you running away again, little devil?" Roarke was suddenly there, his voice in her ear rough and soft at the same time. He pulled her sharply against him, pressing his chest against her back, her shoulders. She gasped, despite herself. His hand closed around her throat, lightly but impossible to evade. He held her still, captive.

She should have hated it.

"I thought we talked about this," he continued.

Every nerve in her body rioted. Fire kindled; barricades burned. Not at what he was doing, but at the fear that he might stop. Her skin prickled with desire, anticipation.

"Answer me, Tessa."

She wasn't entirely sure she could form words at all. She *had* been running away. Not because she did not want him—quite the opposite. She would have run right into his arms if she'd allowed herself. If the thought had occurred to her.

"I'll tell you what," he said. "I'll give you a choice. If you run back into the house, I'll let you be. But if you run into the maze, I'll know you want me to chase you." A forbidden thrill went through her. "I'll know you want me to catch you."

She swayed slightly against him. His teeth grazed her earlobe.

"Right or left, Tessa?" he demanded softly. "Maze or mansion?"

She knew she was already caught.

When he released her, she stumbled.

Then she ran.

Chapter Twenty

SHE CHOSE THE maze.

And, in so choosing, discovered you could run away from something and run *toward* something at the very same time. It was a heady discovery. One worth thinking about.

Later.

She wasn't convinced she was capable of coherent thought right now, and Roarke was not even touching her. He was merely behind her, a suggestion in the shadows, the sound of footsteps. Even, unhurried.

Coming for her.

The air burned in her lungs and her legs quivered as she ran. It was freeing, exhilarating. It released the anxiety and allowed something else to replace it.

It was like jumping into a fire to put out a flame.

But she was already burning. She was always burning with need and want and impossible hope when he was near. Why not let it burn away her loneliness, her doubt? There were so many different ways of caring for one another. Running. Being caught.

Knowing that she was wanted, if only for that moment.

That he was utterly focused on her and did not find her wanting. If only for that moment.

She darted into the maze, half laughing, half catching her breath. The yew hedges rose high on either side of her, blocking out the house, the ball, everything.

Everything but Roarke.

Torches extended above the highest branches, casting just enough light to make it feel as though she was running through honey, through a painting. The ground was hard under her feet, and she turned right because there was no room left for strategy. She turned left and kept going. Roarke was behind her. She did not feel hunted. She felt protected.

Wanted.

Clouds drifted across the moon and the breeze shifted, scented with flowers and the promise of a storm. She turned left.

And abruptly, there was nowhere else to go.

The maze had swallowed her. There were only green needles and thick grass and her own heart pounding in her chest. A decorative bench with a pergola dripping with roses.

And Roarke.

Always Roarke.

He didn't speak, only crossed the distance between them. She didn't have time to turn around. He was just there behind her, pressing into her, mouth on her neck until she arched back, feeling too much. He was hard against her, grinding against the softness of her bottom. Heat bolted down to her quim, throbbing wickedly. She nearly sobbed, and he'd barely touched her.

She was frantic to get her out of her gown, and he was already lifting it up, already running his strong, warm hand up her thighs. His fingers dipped into her, and she was wet, waiting. He growled his pleasure, just a little. Just enough.

"What will make you stay, Tessa?" he said, sliding another finger inside her, pumping into her until she didn't know how long her legs would hold out. "How many times do I have to make you come? Shall we find out?"

She angled toward him, offered like a gift. Desperate. Chasing that friction, that feeling of being filled. *"Roarke."*

"What is it, little devil? What do you want?" The lash of his command made her moan. "Say it."

"You." She was very much afraid she was babbling. She just wanted him inside her, all the way inside her. Now. "More."

He took her hands and curled her fingers around the pergola over the bench to steady her. She still wore her long gloves. "You're going to remember me the next time you run away."

As if she had ever forgotten him. Could ever forget him. That was the problem, wasn't it?

But not tonight. Not right now, when the sky cracked, and the torchlight flickered, and everything felt like a wild dream. When the rain fell, it did not stop them. She did not think anything could have stopped them. And the storm felt right, drops running down her cheeks, down his neck, which she would have followed with her tongue if she could have reached them. The orgasm crashed through her, and she bit into her own arm to strangle the shout.

"Go ahead and scream, little devil," Roarke urged her darkly as the storm lashed all around them, the rain filled every pocket of sound. The lights of the house felt a thousand leagues away. Were the windows open? Would they hear her?

"Go on," he dared her again. "They'll never know. And if they should, all they will know is that you're mine."

His arm banded around her, hauling her closer, pinning her back to his chest. Rain ran into her mouth.

"You can give me another," he commanded. "As many as you can until your legs give out." When they threatened to do just that, his fingers circled her throat, keeping her in place.

He entered her, filling her up with a slow, deep stroke that curled her toes.

Again and again.

His grip on her hips was hard, even as the kisses he dragged across her spine were soft. The combination made her wild. She pushed back against him on every thrust, lifted onto her toes. He pressed his fingers through her slick folds, circling her bud relentlessly until she shivered and quaked and whimpered.

The orgasm tore through her, and he chased it as well, thrusting until he came with a hoarse shout and she came again, caught.

He bit her earlobe, voice feral. "Again."

SHE FOUND SHE could not meet Roarke's eyes at breakfast.

How did one politely acknowledge a person who had feasted on parts of you that still ached for them?

Still, she knew the exact moment he entered her breakfast room, pausing behind her.

The guests had refused to meet her gaze, though for vastly different reasons than hers. They raised their eyebrows, sipped their tea from delicate cups painted with violets, murmured. Always the murmuring.

And then Roarke was there filling the space behind her, and they straightened in their chairs despite themselves. Knives met plates; cups met saucers. She felt him looming behind her, warm and distracting. She sneaked a glance, suddenly feeling shy. And he knew it, given the quiet, amused way he glanced back. And then back to glowering at the glittering guests nursing their sore heads, still swimming with champagne. Their murmurs changed. "Good morning, Lord Dartmoor."

"Lady Dartmoor."

He made them nervous.

A better person might have tried to ease the tension. Tessa just grinned.

"Drink your tea, devil," Roarke said quietly, pulling out her chair before one of the footmen could leap forward.

Someone sighed. Miss Sanditon or Lord Hastings. Not *everyone* feared him. Tessa applauded their taste, even as she feared for her own heart.

It was too early for that nonsense.

Tea. Toasted bread with honey. That was all she needed to focus on. Never mind the ache in her thighs, the sweet soreness from Roarke dragging her into climax after climax.

She reached for her teacup. Lord Falsingham shifted beside

her, trying to put more space between them. Roarke speared him with a glare. He coughed in his hand. "Beg your pardon," he croaked.

Across the table, over a bowl of roses gone soft from an evening spent perfuming the ballroom, Lady Kensington smiled. A huge, bright smile. "Lady Tessa, do try the ham."

If the guests had noted that the marquess had asked her to dance, they also noticed that the marchioness spoke to her like a dear friend. It would have changed her life a year ago. It still made a difference, and she was grateful for it, but she was also grateful not to feel the clawing desperation to change herself, to be perfect, to need the validation. When had that happened? She was far from perfect, and really, wasn't that lovely?

Roarke had never kissed Perfect Tessa.

Anywhere.

And he certainly hadn't taken her in the rain in a maze a hundred feet from the soiree of the Season.

Perfect Tessa's life had been boring. And no more secure for it.

She preferred rusty muskets and nursing cats taking over bedrooms and leaking rooftops. She preferred her candy with a bite of salt. They said that revenge was not ladylike, but they said that because they did not want women to exact revenge. Or justice. Or anything at all.

Tessa took a second portion of ham, scandalizing an elderly viscount.

"Problem, sir?" Roarke asked mildly.

The viscount just shook his head and drank more tea until she feared the man would choke.

Tessa left the table shortly after, more cheerful than she would have thought possible at such an event. Deirdre would have enjoyed the scene.

After breakfast, Tessa found herself in the greenhouse, studying the flowers. She needed just a moment to gather her courage, to screw it to the sticking place now that she had found it.

She wasn't the only one.

A lady approached her, smiling hesitantly, her shoulders squared. Tessa knew that stance intimately. She waited for the lecture on propriety, comments on her *suitability*. For Aunt Celeste to jump out of the bushes.

"Lady Dartmoor?"

Tessa forced a smile, reminding her pulse that this was not worth fussing over. This was not a knife at the throat. Or rabbits eating the last of the lettuce in the garden. Or even Rue's attempt at jellied salad. That was truly a thing to be feared. "Yes?"

"I'm Lady Eleanor. I'm sorry to disturb you." She was tall, with a rosebud mouth and gray eyes. Quite the most beautiful woman Tessa had ever seen. And she was dressed perfectly, from her spotless gloves to the curls falling softly over her ears. Tessa stifled a sigh.

"Not at all."

Fly away, fly away, fly away home.

"Lady Winifred mentioned I should speak with you personally."

Oh.

Everything inside her settled. This she knew. This she understood.

"Is Iri—That is, how is Lady Winifred?"

"Oh, she's fine," Lady Eleanor rushed to assure her. "I'm sorry; I didn't mean to alarm you."

Iris—Winifred—was fine, but Lady Eleanor was clearly nervous. She fiddled with a rose, shredding the petals without noticing. It scented the humid air. "How can I help you?" Tessa asked gently.

"My… friend requires your particular sort of assistance."

"Ah. Your friend." Tessa took a closer look. Lady Eleanor did not appear to be visibly increasing, and nor were there any bruises. That she could see.

Lady Eleanor followed her concerned perusal, and her face cleared. "No, really, I'm here on behalf of a friend. Miss Smith."

"Miss Smith."

"Her actual name, I assure you." She huffed an impatient sigh at herself. "Eleanor, honestly," she muttered. "Miss Smith finds herself with child and without family."

"Without husband, I assume."

"Definitely not." Her brows beetled together. "And I am planning violence."

Tessa grinned. "Now we are getting somewhere. How can I help?"

"Winifred said you might take her in? Help her find alternatives to ruination and orphanages? The viscount in question is willing to take in the child as long as Miss Smith disappears. I don't like the way he says it."

Tessa narrowed her eyes. "I see."

"I think you do. She is my… friend, and I cannot protect her." Frustration laced Lady Eleanor's words, agitated her movements. "He has been to my house three times this week alone. If I take her in right now, it would be the same as advertising her whereabouts."

Tessa nodded once. "Send her to me," she said. "There's a coaching inn not far from Fox Hollow. Send word when she is en route and I will meet her there. I'll need his name, where he keeps house, and any pertinent details you might have. Travel plans would help." The roads were dangerous, after all. There were highwaymen lurking everywhere.

Lady Eleanor grabbed her hands and squeezed them. "You are an angel."

Tessa had to smile. "According to my husband, I am a devil."

Lady Eleanor winked. "Lucky you."

HER LUCK DID not hold out.

"Oh, my lady," one of the maids said when Tessa returned to her chamber. She was clearly stricken, her eyes wide as teacups. "I don't know what happened!"

Tessa knew exactly what had happened. Her chambers had

been tossed. Her dresses lay in heaps on the ground, her shoes scattered in every direction. Pillows were scattered, the mattress half pulled off the frame. The drawers of the pretty escritoire were all open, as were any of the decorative boxes sitting on tables and the mantlepiece. Her necklace and earrings glittered from inside a potted plant, hastily retrieved by another maid.

"I don't think anything is missing." Tessa crouched to right an orchid spilling dirt on the carpet.

"Oh no, my lady, let me." The first maid looked like she might cry.

"It's not your fault," Tessa assured her.

"I don't wish to lose my post. I only just started."

"You won't," she promised firmly. "This wasn't your doing."

"Who would dare? In the marquess's house?" the other maid said. "He'll be furious."

"He doesn't have to know." What would it serve except to heap more scandal onto Tessa's name, and therefore Roarke's? She forced a smile, one she hoped was insouciant but suspected showed far too many teeth. "Perhaps it was a jest."

The first maid narrowed her eyes. "It's not funny."

"No, it really isn't."

"What a terrible mess. We'll have it put to rights by the time you return from the afternoon's entertainments—don't you fret."

As she routinely slept in a room with moss growing on the windowsill, fretting had not occurred to Tessa. Frankly, a small, cowardly part of her would prefer to stay and help tidy up rather than parade around with her you-don't-bother-me smile. Ah well. A small price to pay to be able to properly protect her friends.

But who would do such a thing? Was it personal? Accidental? Merely a fit of pique that she had been welcomed back to Society, if begrudgingly? She wondered if Lord Tewksbury had any relatives at the party. George certainly wouldn't bother—he already had everything of value she had ever possessed.

She had her answer at the bottom of the staircase, where the guests had gathered in their beaver-crowned hats and pelisses for a walk to the garden folly.

Lord Beville.

Her stomach dropped. Did he suspect she had lied to him? Would he return, hunting for Holly despite everything?

She was not the only one who noticed.

Roarke saw her halt. It was just for a moment while she wondered how best to react, if at all. She did not realize how her hand drifted to the cut on her throat, still red, likely to leave a mark.

Roarke noticed.

"Him?" he asked in that dark voice, the one that rumbled like thunder and promised fire.

Tessa swallowed. "I don't—"

"You," Roarke fairly roared, seizing Lord Beville by the necktie and hauling him bodily from the hall.

ROARKE NOTICED THE moment Tessa paused on the stairs, her cheeks going pale.

He took a step forward when they turned red with anger.

When her hand drifted to the delicate skin of her throat and the cut that marred it, he followed her gaze.

After that, it was difficult to remember his thought process. Beyond the kind of cold, simmering rage that made him feel savage. To his bones.

He was the tree cracking in the storm, the ice in spring, the sun on rock. The wasp, the bear. There was nothing of the gentleman left of him.

That man had hurt his wife. *Tessa.*

He had Beville by the throat and sailing into the nearest room before he registered the decision to move. He barely heard the gasps erupt all around him, someone's startled squeak. He released Beville only long enough to slam his fist into the man's face, sending him crashing into a chair and upending on the polished floor. It was satisfying, but nowhere near enough. The man had touched his wife, had tried to hurt her. Had *marked* her.

Tessa was at his heel. "Roarke."

"No use, devil," he said, not taking his eyes from the man groaning and trying to push to his feet. "I saw your face. I know it was him."

She placed her hands on her hips. "I wasn't going to say otherwise." She was. She absolutely was. He could read it in the set of her stubborn chin before he looked back to Beville. "It doesn't matter."

"I'm getting tired of hearing you say that."

She poked his arm. He was threatening the life of a man, and even when he wasn't, he was accustomed to a certain amount of trepidation when people spoke to him. There was blood on his knuckles and murder in his heart, and she *poked* him. "This isn't the place."

"He owes you an apology." His voice darkened. "He owes you blood."

Every drop of Tessa's blood that he had spilled under his knife would be repaid tenfold. A hundredfold. Roarke knew every solitary inch of the moors. They'd never find the body. He'd make certain of it.

Lord Beville, not strong on self-preservation, pushed into a crouch, scowling. Blood spattered his pristine cravat.

Not good enough.

Not nearly good enough.

Lord Beville made a fist, settling into a stance that would be passable in the ring at Gentleman Jackson's.

"I don't think so," Roarke said, and planted him another facer.

Lord Beville had a glass jaw and was not used to resistance of any kind. Not to his title, his estate, his face. He hit the sideboard, rattling the tray of brandy glasses. The decanter tipped over, rolled to the edge, and hit the floor with a smash. Glass skittered like agitated bugs. Roarke already had Tessa held a few inches in the air, protecting her ankles. He set her down gently. The sharpness of spilled liquor punched the air.

"You broke my nose," Beville gasped, shocked.

"It's your jaw next."

"Dartmoor," Kensington said from the doorway, sounding curious and not particularly incensed. At least not over the state of Beville. Over the state of his house was another matter. "Not that I mind a bit of violence," he continued. "But this is my library. I'm rather fond of it. And I was very fond of that decanter. My wife gave it to me."

Lady Kensington peeked over his shoulder. "You hated that decanter."

"It's the principle of the thing."

Roarke planted his boot square on Beville's midsection when the rat tried to scurry away. "Lady Kensington, you should probably leave."

The Marchioness of Kensington, granddaughter to a duke, famous arbiter of fashion and collector of kittens, snorted at him. No wonder she got along so well with Tessa. She closed the door behind them on a sea of nosy guests and footmen. "What's he done?"

"It's nothing," Tessa lied through her teeth.

He was so outraged at the thought of her in danger being *nothing* that he made the kind of strangled sound usually suited to the easily scandalized doyennes of the *ton*. Had he been the type to wear pearls, he would have clutched them. Instead, he set his back teeth and said, very carefully, "He put a knife to your throat."

Kensington went still. "I beg your pardon?"

Lady Kensington sucked in a breath. They both stared at Tessa, at the red mark not quite hidden by the ribbon she wore as a necklace. She smiled weakly. "It's nearly healed."

Lady Kensington turned to Roarke. "In my house?" she asked, incensed. "Hold him down. I want a go."

"A misunderstanding." Lord Beville wiped blood from his lip, but it still stained his teeth. "I did not know she was your wife. It was weeks ago."

"As if that excuses it." Lady Kensington narrowed her eyes.

"And I did tell you I was a countess," Tessa pointed out. She didn't look scared, Roarke was relieved to see. But he was doing a superb job at saving her reputation and clearing her name. She dunked gentlemen in the punch bowl, and he launched them through the library doors. They made quite a team. He couldn't help the small surge of satisfaction, of *knowing*, that went through him.

"I do not like you," Lady Kensington announced, glaring down her nose at Beville. "Consider yourself ostracized."

"Lady K—"

"I suggest you do not address my wife."

"I do like *you*," Lady Kensington said to Roarke. "And I do not wish to see you hanged for murder." She opened the door and motioned to two footmen. "Lord Beville is to be taken to the edge of the laneway and dropped there like the sack of rotten potatoes he is. If he tries to return, you may shoot him for trespassing."

Tessa grinned at her, a cheerful, happy grin best suited to a much younger girl receiving a present on Christmas morning.

Beville recoiled when Roarke approached him where he now hung between two burly footmen. "If I ever see you within a hundred feet of my wife, if you ever look at her again, so much as mention her name, I will end you." Swords shaved every word from him. "Do you believe me, Beville?"

Lord Beville nodded once, jerkily.

"I'll be checking on you," Roarke said as Beville was dragged away. "This isn't over."

A short silence thrummed in the room when they were alone again. Tessa wrinkled her nose. "This is a bit awkward."

Always so forthright. He wanted to kiss her. He contented himself with hauling her up against his side.

Lady Kensington fanned herself. "Well done, Dartmoor. I'm half in love with you myself." Her husband grumbled. She blew him a kiss. "How about a glass of that pear brandy you hide in your desk that you think I don't know about?"

Roarke picked up one of the chairs. The leg had splintered. He felt like a giant again as the fury and adrenaline burned out. "I apologize."

"Don't." Lady Kensington waved her hand. "That was quite invigorating."

"Things were getting boring," Lord Kensington agreed, filling small, fluted glasses painted with cats. "You know how we hate to be boring."

Roarke handed Tessa a glass. She tutted at his knuckles. "You're bleeding."

"Barely."

"Why did he attack you?" Lord Kensington asked her.

"He decided someone he was looking for was living in my house."

"Was she?"

"I've never met the man in my life," she replied, which was not an answer at all.

"I never did like him," Lady Kensington said.

"Then why was he in our house?" her husband asked.

"He wasn't actually invited. My cousin's friend brought him. She thought he might be a suitable match." She set her jaw. "Obviously not." She winced in Tessa's direction. "Do you need a doctor? How frightened you must have been."

She would have been terrified, surely. It iced his blood.

"It's nothing," Tessa assured the marchioness. "A scratch."

Someone growled. Roarke only realized it was him when everyone turned to look at him.

"Goodness," Lady Kensington said, fanning herself again.

"Stop it." Her husband pinched her bottom. She jumped, laughing. "What do we know of this blackguard?"

"He's only just recently come into his title."

"Oh, I remember now. His brother was an absolute nightmare of a man. Both brutish and very high in the instep."

"He was. And his wife was more than half his age, of course.

Pretty, with brown curls, if I recall. She was cheerful but also oddly morbid. There's talk she was carrying the heir."

Roarke's gaze slammed into Tessa.

There was no pretending now. A better, more accurate description of Holly could not be had. Holly, also known as Henrietta, Lady Beville.

"She had not been seen since his death. There are rumors, of course. There are always rumors. The current Lord Beville gets testy when it's brought up." Lady Kensington crossed her arms. "He'd lose everything then, wouldn't he? His title, his wealth. It could not happen to a more deserving man. I believe I shall dedicate myself to that end."

"Please don't," Tessa said quietly. "Men like that shouldn't be underestimated."

She spoke from experience. She knew that fear. He wanted to chase Beville down the lane and break more of his bones.

"I'll take care of it," Roarke promised.

"You... don't have to."

He stared at her. "You're my wife." More than that, she was Tessa.

"But you wanted someone more..." She hesitated, aware they had an audience. "Someone less troublesome."

"I like your trouble just fine." Every word was true. He had promised himself he would keep his distance. That he would never dim her light. But the world was threatening to do just that. And so much worse.

They'd go through him first.

"Never mind," Lady Kensington said cheerfully. "Between the two of you, you've quite made sure this will be the most talked about event of the Season."

"Lord Duncastle will be green with envy." Lord Kensington stopped just short of rubbing his palms together with glee. "He was so smug after he had those doves released inside his ballroom."

"I don't see why." Lady Kensington wrinkled her nose. "It

was spectacularly messy."

"Still, let's see him top this."

Tessa smiled at Roarke. "I like your friends."

He snorted. "You would. Mad, the lot of you."

Chapter Twenty-One

"SO, THIS IS your secret."

They were back in the carriage, opting for a retreat rather than stewing in the cresting gossip and the questions shivering in the air. They'd announced to the world that they were married.

And then proceeded to rip each other's clothes off in the back garden and make a guest bleed in the library.

That had not gone particularly to plan. Even for her.

She was used to plans changing, to adapting, pivoting. She was not used to someone like Roarke coming to her defense. She warned herself not to get used to it. She desperately wanted to get used to it—not to having him ride to her rescue, but to just have him there. To be able to rely on the fact that he would not leave or get bored or send her away.

She also desperately wanted to bite her way across his chest, down his stomach.

"Tessa."

She stifled a sigh. Clearly his mind was elsewhere, while hers was… indecent.

"Yes." There was no sense in lying about it now. She might not elaborate, but he clearly knew Holly was the Dowager Countess Beville. A dowager at twenty-two years old. Her husband had been more than twice her age, more than twice as powerful as her or her family, more than twice as worldly. What options had been left to her when he turned cruel? Violent? And then his brother turned out to be no better. "Please don't tell anyone."

He looked affronted, scowling at her as the carriage wheel dipped into a rut in the road. The glass rattled in the window casing. "Do you think I would?"

"No."

He looked vaguely mollified. "Good."

"But do you see now how it was not my story to tell?"

"I see that it was your house that you took danger into." He was not going to be placated, not over this.

"Was I supposed to do any different?"

"You?" His expression softened. She fought the urge to sit next to him, to breathe in his cedar scent, to feel the weight of his arm around her shoulder. "Never."

"I did once," she said quietly.

"Did what?"

"Look away? For just a moment." She forced her hands not to clench. The view outside the window was all trees and blue skies. She barely saw it. She only saw Deidre excited to be in love, talking of wedding flowers, weeping when Tewksbury ceased talking to her. The muddy alley where she died with her baby. "My friend Deirdre was in a similar strait."

"Tewksbury."

"Yes. He wasn't violent, but he abandoned her. Everyone abandoned her."

"Are you trying to tell me that you abandoned her as well? Because I know for a fact that you could not."

"I should have been there for her. She should have come to me."

His hand closed over hers, warm and comforting. "I'm sure she knew that."

"Instead, they found her body in an alley. I won't let it happen again," she said fiercely, refusing to let the tears fall.

"Hence Magpie House."

"Hence Magpie House." It was the best she could do in the moment. She could not tell him everyone's secrets. Not without permission.

"I understand, you know," he said. "A little. Did Beville believe you that Holly was not in residence?"

"I think so?"

"You're not sure."

"I'm mostly sure."

"I'll have men watch him until the babe is born."

She blinked. "You will?"

"Certainly. And if it's a boy, we can devise a new plan. Something to keep them safe. I'm not convinced he wouldn't murder a child to remain the earl."

Roarke leaned over suddenly, tugging her forward and then onto his lap as the carriage rumbled on. She landed on his thighs. "What are you doing?" She wanted to curl around him like a cat.

He tucked her into his side. "I'm feeling anxious."

"I don't think you are." She peered up at him doubtfully. She could not remember the last time she had been cradled, surrounded by the kind of strength she could rely on. And it was not the physical kind—though she was rather enjoying the hard, warm planes of his body against hers. "And I am not either, if that's what worries you. I don't need to be coddled."

It was a bit nice, though.

"He had a knife to your throat, and I wasn't there," Roarke replied darkly. "I am feeling a great deal more than anxious." He pushed her head gently down onto his shoulder. "Now hush."

She bit back a smile. "Yes, Lord Dartmoor."

"Roarke," he growled into her hair. "You call me Roarke."

She would have, had she not already been drifting off, warm and comfortable. She felt his lips in her hair, his arms tightening around her.

"Sleep," he murmured. "I've got you."

WHEN NONI CAME bustling down the stairs with a basket of cloths, Tessa knew the Kensingtons' was not the only house party to offer surprises.

"Holly?" she asked immediately.

"Perfectly well," Noni assured her and Roarke. "The babe came last night, a couple of weeks early but nothing to fret over." A tiny, incensed wail drifted down behind her. She smiled. "Very strong."

Tessa darted up the stairs, Roarke behind her. "Thank you, Noni," she tossed over her shoulder.

"Don't let her eat any more pickled cucumbers!"

"I'd as soon be able to stop the sunset," Tessa muttered as they came to Holly's room.

She was sitting up in bed, a bright smile on her exhausted face and a tiny, fussy bundle in her arms. Rue perched beside her, hair coming out of her pins, eyes also tired but happy. Fergus stood behind, proud as a peacock. They made quite the picture. Tessa saw the way they leaned toward each other, the care and affection that glittered like a silver ribbon winding around and between them. Interesting. Unexpected.

"I was barely away two days," Tessa teased.

"She could not wait," Holly replied.

"She?" Relief released the knot in her stomach. "Do you mind very much? Not having an estate or an inheritance for her?"

Holly shook her head, tracing her daughter's tiny nose. "If she'd been a boy there would have been a target on his back for his entire life. But Beville does not care about girls."

"Roarke punched Beville in the face and broke his nose," Tessa offered cheerfully.

Holly's eyes misted. "What a lovely birthday present for her. I shall tell her about it when she is older. Every year on this day."

Roarke's ears went ruddy. It was so endearing that Tessa couldn't help but beam. Not enough people saw this side of him.

"But I'm not naming her Fennel," Holly muttered. "No matter how Marigold begs." She paused. "Comfrey, perhaps."

Rue's expression dared them all to react. To say a single thing that was not enthusiastically complimentary. Even as she stifled an eye roll. Or two.

"Parsley and Comfrey," she said. "They shall be like sisters."

As Holly's eyelids began to droop, Rue ushered them away. She stopped Tessa in the hall. "A word?"

They stepped into another room that had once been lemon yellow and was now more on par with mustard. That had sat in the sun for too long. "Gah," Tessa said. "No wonder no one ever comes in here."

"Only someone has," Rue said, tone full of needles and vinegar and foreboding.

Tessa frowned. "In here?"

"Everywhere."

"The weasel?"

"No weasel I know is capable of opening windows or moving furniture."

"Blast," Tessa said. "Perhaps Beville is behind it?"

"He was with you, was he not? And why would he be interested in going through the cupboards?"

"Good point." She rubbed her face. "That leaves your earl, Marigold's jackass, or whoever Bryony is hiding from."

"I did ask her this morning."

Tessa's eyes widened. "And did she tell you?"

"Of course not. But she seemed confident this has nothing to do with her."

"Do the others know?"

"I didn't want to alarm them." Tessa raised an eyebrow. Rue *frequently* wanted to alarm them. "Oh, very well—I was busy with Holly. She was having a baby, after all."

"Someone from the village, then? One can hope."

"Mayhap. They might think this a very fine house." They exchanged a glance. "More fool they," Rue added, patting the wall with affection. Her hand came away damp. "Repulsive."

"I shall see about more footmen," Tessa said. "To keep

watch. And I'll talk to Peter in the gatehouse. After I wipe these walls with vinegar."

Rue dragged her hand down her skirt, nose wrinkling. "Please do."

Tessa spent the rest of the day stripping wallpaper and scraping moss and swatting at cobwebs. She found letters from the downstairs parlor in the upstairs parlor. Decorative boxes with their rusted lids pried open. A strongbox under a bed bearing what were definitely scorch marks. Recent? Or the result of some other nosy housebreaker a hundred years ago?

She also found porcelain sheep scattered in pieces on the floor, Paulette weeping over them.

"Oh, my lady!" she hiccupped, jumping when Tessa found her on her knees with a dustpan. "I'm so sorry. I didn't see them there on the edge of the table."

Tessa smiled gently. They were all aware of how delicate Paulette was, bursting into tears at the slightest provocation, constantly looking over her shoulder, jumping at every sound. Tessa did not pry. But she knew a woman in hiding when she saw one. "Don't trouble yourself," she said. "There used to be dozens of those insipid things. I thought we'd already smashed them all playing bowls."

Paulette blinked. "Oh."

Tessa glanced around, noting the general disarray. "I see the weasel has made himself comfortable in here as well."

She didn't mention the floorboard, partially pulled up. Rue was right—Tessa did not know of any weasels who could do that. Someone had definitely been going through the house. How had they managed it, unseen by Mrs. Pompadour's eagle eye and her suspicious footmen? Lennox paced the halls at all hours, soothing Parsley. Someone was nearly always awake.

Paulette wiped at the floor, taking away the ceramic shards and a layer of grime. Underneath, beautiful red cabbage roses had been painted directly on the wood. "See? Another surprise in this house," Tessa said. "And all it took was a few sheep."

"I'll wash it up straightaway, my lady."

TESSA DID NOT see much of Roarke until later that night. He spent hours with Peter, Lennox, and Fergus assessing the security of windows and doors, discussing new locks, generally acting as though they were under siege. And he did not even know about the rooms that had been tossed. Tessa did not remind him that they had already checked all of the ways in and out of the house, and that there were a few secret doors he did not even know about. There were bells attached to the lower-floor entrances.

She wasn't about to turn down help if it would keep her friends safe.

They met at midnight, in the kitchen, as was their habit. This time it wasn't just for wine or leftover cake. Holly was still in bed, but the others sat around the table in their shawls and night shifts. Rue poured thick brown ale into mugs.

"Ale," Daphne said before taking a sip. "That's never a good sign."

"We have a weasel," Rue said, finally taking her seat.

"We also have several feral cats, a badger, and a nest of starlings in the ballroom," Daphne pointed out. "And a spider roughly the size of a donkey in the back hall."

"Not that kind of weasel, I'm afraid," Tessa said. She plucked the list of names off the wall where it was still secured by a rusty dagger salvaged from the attic. *Lord Beville, Viscount Eastbourne, Lord Wrexham.*

Bryony froze. "What do you mean?"

"Someone has been going through the house, rifling through the belongings." Tessa helped herself to a biscuit with pink icing. Fergus had learned to color sugar icing with raspberry juice because Rue secretly liked pink. It was rather sweet. If she mentioned it, though, Rue was likely to pelt her with those same biscuits, and that would be a waste.

Daphne frowned. "Not the servants, surely."

"No, I doubt that very much. But weasels also don't move

furniture and pry up broken floorboards."

"That sounds as though someone is looking for a thing and not a person?" Bryony suggested. Her shoulders were still stiff, but they loosened slightly.

"I know you won't tell us who you are hiding from," Tessa said gently. "But could he be behind this? Or she? They?"

Bryony shook her head. "The house would already be burning to the ground if *he* were here."

Daphne gulped. "Bollocks."

Tessa lifted an eyebrow at her, trying to lighten some of the tension even as it wrapped around her. "You did not learn that word in a Mayfair ballroom."

"I learned it here." Daphne snorted. "Obviously."

"Obviously."

Rue frowned, brushing crumbs off her fingers. "I don't think it would be the Earl of Wrexham after me, either," she said. "It's not his style."

Tessa nodded. "I'll make inquiries, just in case. Perhaps Summer has heard something about his current whereabouts."

"And the viscount already knows where I am," Marigold yawned. "He's always known where I lived, and it did not matter then. I don't know why it would now."

Tessa winced. "Probably not." She sighed. "It doesn't make sense, then."

"It might be nothing," Daphne suggested. She sounded hopeful but not convinced.

"Mayhap," Tessa said.

Rue snorted. "It's always something."

Unfortunately, she wasn't wrong.

"We've dealt with worse," Tessa said. "We don't falter." She toasted them with her ale. "Stand and deliver."

They lifted their mugs in salute. "Stand and deliver."

Chapter Twenty-Two

SHE WAS IN her bedchamber when the knock came at the connecting door.

"Come in."

The door handle turned, stuck. Turned again. There was a muffled curse and then a loud crash as Roarke used his shoulder to force it open. The frame splintered slightly, and the swollen wood and thick layers of paint protested.

"That door has not been opened in years," Roarke said. He was in his shirt sleeves, collar open at this throat, cravat long since discarded. The candlelight made him look like Hercules standing in the lion's den, all muscles and gold light. He studied her for a long moment, seeming to come to a decision. About what, she did not know. "I have a question about my room."

She blinked. "All right."

"Why are there so many grapes in there? I can't tell if I'm queasy or hungry."

"I forgot we put you in the Grape Room."

"You said it was the Blackbird Room."

"One day, it shall be." She peeked behind him. The moldings were ornamented with grapes, bunches growing in the corners, trailing over the door lintels. Painted on the walls, choking the ceiling. All in the most unfortunate shade of vermillion green. "Eventually."

"I suspect one of the previous owners was a bit of a drunk," Roarke said, leaning close as though he were confessing.

"We can move you?" Tessa suggested. Unless he was not staying for long. They had not discussed it. She would not ask. Not tonight. Tomorrow she would be brave. "We have a lovely blue room. You'll feel like you're underwater."

"Seasick, you mean," he said with a brief smile.

She thought of the many mirrors in the chamber, of the blue coverlet embroidered with a wave pattern, of the seashells pressed into the wall. Of the exceedingly odd perspective of the mural of a mermaid who may or may not have three arms. "That too."

"I'll deal with the grapes, thank you very much."

She worried at her bottom lip, suddenly not sure what to say. What to do.

"You've been cooped up all day," Roarke said. "And so have I. How about a walk?"

She nodded. He plucked her shawl from the back of a chair and handed it to her. She was decidedly less neat than she had been with a lady's maid to tidy up behind her. There were teacups on the table again. Two pairs of muddy boots on the floor. And she was reasonably certain that countesses generally did not have stacks of mouse-nibbled books on the floor, or a vase filled with sticks and an antique dagger. Roarke didn't seem to mind; he walked past her to open the door and motion for her to precede him.

He changed when he was outside—she could see it in the lines at the corners of his eyes, the line of his jaw. He had always disdained drawing rooms for the fields. Candlelight for moonlight. She hadn't truly understood that about him before. She should have, as she also preferred it. She hadn't realized that about herself either, not until the last few months.

Tonight was a perfect example. She'd been restless and distracted all day, filling her hours with work. Tonight had started the same, until Roarke led her through the garden under the moonlight. The flowers were nearing their last bloom, decadent and excessive and wilting under the weight of their own beauty. The air was cool, smelling of damp and loam and the smoke from someone's fire down in the village. Crickets and grasshoppers competed in song, trilling in the long grasses beyond the garden wall.

"What did you do today?" he asked.

"A thousand things," Tessa replied. "And I went down to the village."

He sent her a sidelong glance. "And how was it?" he asked, too casually. "How was Mrs. Harris?"

"Mrs. Harris was the soul of nervous civility." She paused. "*What* did you do?"

He grunted.

She stopped walking. "Roarke Noble."

He only smiled a little at her governess tone. "I merely reminded the good shopkeepers of Fox Hollow that if they did not wish to keep shop, they certainly didn't have to."

"I don't even know how that's a threat, but I am certain it is." It wouldn't have been what he said, more the towering hulk of him, the sudden sharpness in those leaf-green eyes. No wonder Madame Colette's had all but cleared when she'd stepped inside. Madame Colette had offered her tea, coffee, and even a wedge of cheese in increasing agitation. Mrs. Harris had curtsied, bright red in the face, and could not meet her gaze. "You probably should not terrorize the village folk," she said drily.

He shrugged, unconcerned. "I stop when they stop. Although I suppose I do owe you an apology. For yesterday." The gravel walk crunched under his shoes. "I did not mean to embarrass you," he said gruffly. "At the Kensingtons'."

"You didn't embarrass me."

He looked as surprised by her nonchalance as she was by his concern. "I planted a facer on an earl."

"On a jackass, you mean."

He grinned. "Also true. But still not exactly ballroom etiquette."

She shrugged one shoulder. "If he wants to be treated courteously, he ought to act with courtesy."

"You're really not upset?"

"Roarke, I held *you* up with a pistol."

"That tiny antique? I'm surprised it even works."

She wrinkled her nose because he was not wrong. "That's not the point."

"If you're going to go about breaking the law and threatening unscrupulous men, you should have a working weapon."

He wasn't suggesting she stop holding up carriages. Which any reasonable person would be excused for requesting. Demanding even. He only wanted her to have better resources on hand. He did not seem to want her to change back to the Tessa who floated through art galleries and tea parties and danced until dawn in Vauxhall Gardens.

And she loved him for it.

She *loved* him.

Damnation.

Well, that was certainly inconvenient.

One did not fall in love with one's husband. Especially when the contract practically forbade it. He did not want a wife. Not really.

And that mattered not at all to her inconvenient heart.

She wanted him to stay with her at Magpie House. To sleep in a room overdecorated with grapes and sit in chairs by the fire when the damp wormed its way through the walls. She wanted to wake up next to his warmth, the hardness of him along her body, his breath in her air.

She *wanted.*

Him. Only him.

And wanting was so dangerous.

But she had already decided she would be brave tomorrow. Tomorrow was for words and decisions. Not tonight. Not now.

She slipped her hand in his and tugged him between the

mulberry trees and the wild roses climbing along every available surface. Under a curtain of ivy, back into the house and up the stairs toward her bedroom. Whatever happened after tonight, she wanted a memory of him in her bed. The smell of him on her pillows. The indentation of him in the soft and not particularly comfortable mattress.

His eyes flared, not looking away when she walked backward, pulling him in her wake. The air was charged, heated. She lit a single candle, just enough to see him by, not enough to break that feeling of a safe and secret cocoon just for the two of them. Her fingers trembled. He clasped her wrist, taking the candle and the matchstick from her. Lighting it, placing it on the windowsill, and then turning back to her.

She dropped her shawl, and then pulled the ribbon at the neckline of her night shift. It held most of it together, not being particularly new. She did not mind this time, for it fell to her feet, and his gaze raked over her. Lust prickled her skin. He rubbed a hand over his jaw. "Come here."

She hesitated, only to see what he would do. Only to feel that thrill, that knowledge inside of her body. His touch before he even touched her.

His voice dropped to a harsh demand. "Come here, Tessa. Or I'll come to you."

She nearly moaned.

"Is that what you want?" he asked, prowling toward her. The evidence of his arousal pressed against the fall of his breeches, hard, insistent. She wanted to touch him, to feel him, taste him.

She lowered to her knees.

He stilled, cursing under his breath. "Tessa."

"You come to me, Roarke," she whispered. She licked her lips.

"You're trying to kill me, devil."

She looked up at him through her lashes. He was just a little unsteady as she approached her, clearly leashing his control the way you would leash a tiger—carefully, with a firm hand. Hers fumbled at his buttons, but only for a moment. The fierce desire in his face emboldened her. Heat gathered, pooling wetness between her thighs. She pressed them together. He groaned. She finally worked the buttons free and dragged his breeches down to his ankles. He kicked them free, standing over her, proud, naked, silk over steel.

She'd never felt smaller.

Or larger than life.

She ran her fingers up his thighs, and his hair tickled her skin; his muscles flexed under her palms. She leaned forward and licked along his length, base to tip. When he staggered slightly, his hand ghosting over her head, a groan trapped in his throat, she took the length of him in her mouth without warning and sucked hard. His groan turned to a harsh shout, harsher pants. She sucked again and again, raking her nails gently over him, cradling the rest of him that would not fit in her mouth. His hips stuttered. "*Fuck*, Tessa."

And then suddenly he had hauled her to her feet and his mouth seized hers, desperate, starving, just a bit rough. That tiger prowled between them. He dragged her over his length, pressing his cock into her warmth. She rubbed against him, angling for more, moaning. The sound she made undid him. His fingers dug into her hair, into her hip, and his teeth were on her throat; his tongue licked away the sting, deepening it, sending arrows of want between her legs. She throbbed with it. He pushed her onto her back, the messy sheets swallowing them. The hardness of him pressed into her, top to bottom. It wasn't enough. Would never be enough.

"Tessa?" he growled into her temple.

"Yes?" It was *yes*; every part of her screamed *yes*.

"This mattress is atrocious."

She laughed, she couldn't help it. "I know. But we have expectant mothers who deserve soft beds. And not enough coin." Not until they'd married. But she didn't want to talk about that, not now.

"So do you. You deserve a soft bed."

"I can wait." She didn't care about soft beds, not now. She squirmed beneath him, gasping at the nudge of his cock between her lips.

He caught her chin, handsome face going hard. "No. You deserve as much as anyone else. *More.*"

"I want more of *you,*" she said, frustration licking at her blood. She bit his shoulder.

He huffed a laugh. "Poor devil," he murmured, moving his fingers along her thigh, grazing her heat. "Is there something you needed?"

She widened her legs, and they both panted.

"Am I neglecting you?" he whispered in her ear. He stroked the crease of her thigh, teasing. Tormenting. The hair of his chest tickled her spine.

"Roarke," she very nearly begged. *"Please."*

He slid two fingers inside her, without mercy, rubbing her inner walls, pulling free, plunging deep again. The sudden sensations stole her words, threatening to steal her breath. He was relentless, chasing her pleasure as it built, rubbing his thumb over her bed, a soft touch, a hard circle. When her back arched, he followed. And when her orgasm finally released, he pulled back just long enough to drive his cock into her, and her wet heat clenched around him. Her moans were strangled. "Fuck," he groaned. *"Finally."*

A second climax went through Tessa, surprising her, soft where the first had been relentless. Long and languid, turning her bones to liquid heat.

Roarke nudged her to her side, slipping his knee between her legs. He gripped her thigh and slid back into her slowly, so slowly. The pressure of his filling her sent sparks through her belly, made her legs tremble. He rubbed her nipple, squeezing her breast, lightly pulling the tip—refusing to let the fire collapse to coals; refusing anything that was not her body. His mouth moved gently under her ear, and his breath stirred the curls there.

It was slow and perfect and desperately intimate. There was no hiding, no running. He was everywhere.

She moved with him, pushing back until he went even deeper, until their breathing turned harsh. "Not yet, not yet," he said. "Come for me again, one more. *One more.*"

He circled her bud, small circles, bigger circles, alternating until she couldn't predict him, until she could only fall into the moment and burn. He caught her, fell with her in slow, deep thrusts until he came with her name on his lips.

Chapter Twenty-Three

WHEN TESSA RETURNED to her room at dawn, something was off.

She didn't notice at first; she was too hazy with sleep and the pleasant ache in her body reminding her of how she had spent the last few hours. Her lips were slightly swollen from Roarke's kisses, chafed by his beard, just like her inner thighs. They had snuck down to the kitchen for leftover pudding, which Roarke had eaten from between her breasts. They had paused in the music room and continued to devour each other in Roarke's bed until she was so weak from pleasure that she fell asleep.

And then woke up starving. She was half surprised that Roarke did not also wake to the rumbling of her belly. She moved slowly, careful not to wake him. There was a basket of apples and pears and nuts in her room. She had adopted Summer's habit of hiding food in case Rue was in a fit of temper in the kitchens.

But now she was in her room, and it felt cold and dusty, and she missed the heavy weight of Roarke's arm draped over her. Even the awful acidic-green glow of painted grapes.

But it was more than that.

She frowned, wondering what she was missing.

When she realized what it was, equal parts confusion and dread settled like a stone in her stomach. The doors of the wardrobe across from the bed were open. It didn't mean much at first glance; the latch was a bit temperamental. And though she was not as neat as she could be, she also knew she had not dumped *all* of her shoes onto the floor.

Someone had been in her room.

Sometime between her sneaking out to the kitchen with Roarke and now.

She shifted, ready to sound the alarm. But she noticed her green boots, the ones she had taken to hiding her father's watch inside of after the first housebreaker, tossed with the others. Worse, when she grabbed the left boot, the watch was gone.

Her father's watch was gone.

Not just gone. Taken. Deliberately.

She could not make sense of it. Did not have time to. Because in its place was a rolled-up scrap of parchment. She scanned it, going cold.

Lady Winifred Eaton.

Lady Fontescu.

Lady Beville.

Miss Weatherby.

The paper trembled in her grip. Icy sweat gathered at the base of her skull.

Iris.

Rue.

Holly.

Bryony.

She felt sick. Someone knew the identities of everyone at Magpie House. The threat was clear. And still she stayed silent, struck dumb. She wanted to scream, wanted to ring the bell. Anything.

She didn't.

Go to the crossroads past the bridge. Tell no one or I tell everyone.

She moved like an automaton, half frozen, half jumping ahead to every option she could think of. Which were very few. The best she could do was buy time. She dressed quickly, slipped on those green half-boots, and left Magpie House before the sun had finished climbing over the horizon. She stopped long enough to slip a note under Rue's door. She also slipped a dagger in each boot and tucked one into her stays. Roarke would no doubt be furious that she did not wake him, but if she had, he'd be walking by her side.

If he didn't tie her to a chair instead.

This was her responsibility. She had made promises. Her friends deserved to be safe. And she had no idea why her father's pocket watch might endanger them. Why her very presence might suddenly be a risk. She did know she would get it back. And she would destroy whoever was threatening them. She assumed they wanted money. It had to be simple blackmail. But why her? Why now?

None of it made any sense.

The morning was far too beautiful for the rage she felt inside her chest. Dew sparkled in the tall grass; birds sang with their whole little feathered chests. The wind smelled of fallen apples and rain. She hurried, the hem of her dress growing damp, her nose cold. She was no closer to figuring out who would want her old family keepsake.

And she was out of time.

"I had so hoped you'd be reasonable," a man said from behind her. "But I did not count on it. I am happy to be surprised, cousin."

George.

She whirled, curses on the tongue, no less confused.

But he was already on her, stuffing a sweet-smelling rag over her nose and mouth.

SHE WOKE INSIDE a carriage.

She was slumped in the corner, her hands tied together.

"You're awake," George said, sounding annoyed that she had made him wait.

She tried to kick him, but the very large footman sitting beside him stopped her. The force of it reverberated through her teeth. She sat up, vision blurring. "Are you resorting to abducting women now?"

"I would be nicer to me, were I you," George said, moving away as if her very presence would sully him. "I hold all of the cards."

"I hope I am sick all over your boots," she muttered. Which was a distinct possibility. She did not feel well. The carriage wobbled, making matters worse. She swallowed thickly.

"Don't you dare," he said, sounding panicked for the first time.

"It's your fault for drugging me," she snapped. "Was that laudanum?" She hated laudanum. It made her head swim and her mouth feel woolly. She hadn't touched a drop since she'd broken her wrist as a child. She took slow, deep breaths through her nose. It helped a little. "Where are we going?"

"Bath."

"What the hell for?"

He clucked his tongue. "That is not how a lady speaks."

"Oh, I do beg your pardon, you *absolute jackass*."

She sat up fully, feeling a bit stronger. She eyed the footman. He was nowhere near as wide as Roarke was, but he did not appear even half as friendly. She was not going to be able to overpower him. If she went for one of her daggers now, he would no doubt beat her to it.

She pressed a hand to her temple, willing it to stop throbbing. It almost worked. "George, what could you possibly want with my father's old watch? You already have everything."

And how did he know about the women living in her house? She wanted to demand he tell her, but she wasn't sure if it gave him all of the power. Though she supposed she had already admitted as much by meeting him in the first place.

"You really don't know?" he asked, watching her with narrowed eyes.

She made a sound of disgust. "No, I don't."

"You hummed the little tune it plays at me at the Kensingtons'. Ridiculous couple."

She felt rather protective of that ridiculous couple, and so she bared her teeth.

"I was humming to help me keep my temper," she said. "Because you are an odious little cretin." Her eyes widened. "You were the one who went through my room," she realized. Is that what you were looking for? The watch? Why not just ask me?"

"I might have, but your mountain of a husband would not let me near you after the disgusting display with Beville."

"You stole my dowry. I was barely allowed to pack my own dresses and a single toy when I was nine years old. The watch is all I have left."

"I need it."

"Why? Whatever for?"

"You'll find out soon enough."

"Oh, lovely. Are you trying to be mysterious now?"

"No more so than you, with your house full of fallen women and soiled doves."

She pinched the bridge of her nose. "Oh, sod off."

He stiffened. "Mind yourself, cousin."

"Those women deserve your respect, if only because they have had to put up with spoiled, selfish, cowardly men like you their entire lives."

George flicked his hand at the footman. "I do not like her manners."

The footman leaned forward with the kind of excited gleam in his eye that made her sick to her stomach, even without the laudanum. He enjoyed this kind of bullying work. She knew it before he grabbed her arm, bruising the flesh almost instantly. Then he shoved her hard, so that her head hit the window. Pain lanced through her. She clenched her jaws against the roll of nausea.

"Now that we understand each other," George said, wiping imaginary dust off his sleeve, "tell me about the watch."

"There's nothing to tell. My father always carried it with

him."

"Where did he get it?"

"How should I know? I was barely out of the nursery when he used to sing me the song it played." She had no idea if he'd bought the watch because of the song or if he sang her the song because of the watch.

"You'd better hope for your own sake that your memory sharpens. Because we're here."

The carriage rumbled to a stop.

TESSA HAD RUN away.

Again.

It was bad enough that when Roarke woke, his bed was empty. He wanted her snug bottom against him, her hair tangled on his pillow. Cold feet because she stole all of the blankets. Mercilessly.

Not this cold, empty feeling in his chest.

It only got worse when he found her bed empty, her clothes on the floor.

Her daggers missing.

He'd been trying to convince himself that he was being dramatic. That he'd spent too much time with the theatrical Lord Kensington, with Holly and her morbid poetry, with Rue and her kitchen knife. In a house rigged to take out guests with swinging chandeliers and trick stairs. He was accustomed to the moors, to wild ponies and very few people, and those people were generally too intimidated to look him in the eye, never mind chatter on about the logic behind nicknaming Tessa Punch Bowl Ophelia.

He'd chosen this because it fulfilled an oath to his dying mother.

His very clever, very troublesome mother.

She had not cared for his first wife. She had mourned her death, as was proper and compassionate, but not the death of his marriage to a woman who had run away to be with any man but him. All other men. A woman who had hated the quiet of the country, hated long walks outside, mud on her boots, a hulking husband who did not know any poetry and would not wear cravats unless forced by king or Parliament. He was not elegant, entertaining.

And now Tessa.

Gone.

But she wouldn't leave, not like this. That much he knew, even if his heart was racing and in very great danger of cracking into pieces like those damned ceramic animals they used to play at bowls. The hallway was littered with the dust.

She wouldn't leave the women of Magpie House.

Whatever his uncertainties and worries, that much was true. She might have left *him*. He wanted to howl at the sky at the thought. But she wouldn't leave *them* without a word, without a plan. She wouldn't leave this disaster of a house. She'd kick him out on his arse first.

Even if she had snuck out of his bed on their wedding night and run away.

He rubbed his chest. None of this felt right. Not her leaving; not the prickle across the back of his neck.

He pulled on a shirt and prowled through the house, in case she was tucked away somewhere, scraping paint off a two-hundred-year-old table. Pulling rusty nails from a cracked banister. Chasing the weasel out of the music room, where it sometimes liked to dance across the pianoforte keys, creating the most discordant song. She always laughed. Yesterday he had stood on the stairs, arrested by that laugh. Frozen like a lovesick fool, grinning at nothing.

She wasn't anywhere to be found. Not the kitchen after a toasted muffin, nor the gardens for lavender to rub on a splinter.

There had been too many housebreakers, too many men with knives and plans for him to feel at ease.

Rue marched toward him, a letter in her hand. "We have a problem."

Chapter Twenty-Four

THE HOUSE WAS grand in the way only a house in Bath could be, with balconets and columns and black iron railings. She had never been to the Crescent, never seen the half-moon of terraced houses made of the golden stone overlooking the parkland. She had never been to this house with the blue door and the lark knocker.

But she knew it all the same. It was familiar in a way that she could not explain.

She knew the floors in the front hall were pink marble, and the slender columns on either side of the grand staircase were painted gold. There were yellow roses in the garden outside the window and birdcages scattered throughout the parlor.

Her father's lullaby played in her head. *I'll gather you roses by the back door, as gold as your hair. One for you, and one for me, and one for little lark.*

This was her mother's house. Lark House.

She faltered on the front step. She'd been so little the last time she was here that she had forgotten the birdcages, the smell of lemon polish. She only remembered it because of the lullaby, and the stories her father told her. He'd stopped coming here after her mother died. She only remembered it because it came flooding back to her, like a river rushing its banks.

This might have been her only moment to shout for help.

Carriages trundled loudly behind them; visitors and neighbors strolled the famous street, nodding to each other. Bath bustled with life, and the Crescent was the epicenter of fine Society, when they were not out taking the famous waters. Half a dozen people could look up to see her right now, but George had thrown a cloak over her shoulders, and it fell over her bound hands. By the time she shook herself free of the shock of recognizing her mother's house, of the lullaby in her head, it was too late.

The footman had already hauled her inside, slamming the door shut.

Wake up, Tessa, she scolded herself. The laudanum was starting to fade from her system. She needed to figure out what George was doing and how to stop him. How to get out of here.

She opened her mouth to scream. The footman's sweaty hand clamped over her mouth and nose, strangling her.

"Don't bother," George said. "The servants are all gone on a week's holiday and won't hear you. But I don't care for the caterwauling."

She'd give him caterwauling.

She'd been tricked by George Kilkenny. The man who could not tie his own cravat without assistance. Who had never rinsed a plate or dusted a cobweb.

It was both infuriating and embarrassing.

"I still don't know what you want from me," she said. The floor was pink marble under her boots, as predicted. She nearly smiled. Might have, if the footman hadn't been pushing into her personal space with the kind of leer that bullies seemed to learn from birth.

"You're going to show me where the family strongbox is," George replied.

She stared at him. "And you needed my father's watch for this?" Tessa tilted her head, all false concern. She probably shouldn't antagonize him, but she couldn't help it. He wouldn't get an ounce of her fear. He would get drunk on it. "Are you feeling quite well, George?"

He took the watch from his pocket and slammed it down on the nearest table. The glass cracked.

Tessa couldn't help a sound of distress. "Don't."

"Where is it?" he screamed, spittle flying from his mouth.

She took a step back and bumped into the grinning footman. "I don't know," she said, as calmly as she could. "How could I? I haven't been here since I was in leading strings."

"He must have told you."

She frowned. "My father? Why would he? What's inside the strongbox?" She shook her head. "Is this about jewels? I doubt he had any that you haven't already claimed."

If this was about jewels, she was going to be so angry.

Angrier than she already was.

"Find. It." He was losing what little control he had on his temper. The footman started to look sickeningly eager.

"All right, George," she said, clenching her hands so they wouldn't see her fingers shake.

She circled the study first, peering behind books, feeling under the desk. She lifted the edge of the carpet.

"Don't you think we've tried all that?" George snapped.

She bit back a retort involving the capacity of his mind and the general state of his bollocks. Probably not helpful. She moved to the largest drawing room next. The large sash windows were curtained with blue velvet. She peeked behind them. Nothing. The moldings dripped with details, leaves and fat flowers and tiny larks in flight. It was a grand house, clearly well situated. It would cost a fortune to keep. To buy.

She paused.

George's greed was well documented. But she still could not understand what this might have to do with her or her father's watch. Unless the house was not entailed? Surely someone would have said something before now, even accidentally.

The footman hulked behind her, his breath excited. She swallowed a wave of nausea and stepped aside. "If you want to solve this little mystery, you'll have to call off your dog. He smells like boiled celery that's gone off. It's distracting."

His lips lifted off his teeth. George waved his hand. "You'll have your chance if she doesn't deliver."

She pushed down the fear the way she always did.

With a lullaby.

I'll gather you roses by the back door, as gold as your hair. One for you, and one for me, and one for little lark.

Fly high or fly low, wherever you go, the moon keep you, little lark. The sun keep you, little lark, and yellow roses for your hair.

Fly away, fly away, fly away home.

It wasn't nonsense after all. It wasn't poetry or a fairy tale or a lullaby.

It was a clue.

Just for her.

Her father might not have known his young nephew would turn out the way he did, but he certainly knew enough about his sister not to trust her or her mothering.

And yellow roses for your hair.

That was very specific. So she would start there. She turned on her heel and marched toward the back door and the very prolific yellow roses she was unsurprised to find pushing at the glass. She didn't realize she was still humming under her breath until she saw that it made George anxious.

She hummed louder.

"Stop it."

"Do you want me to find this strongbox, or not?"

The door with the roses was in a music room, used at dinner parties for ladies to display their talents at the pianoforte or harpsichord. She had been in dozens of rooms just like this, singing and playing music to entertain bored guests, either flirting behind their fans or dozing from too much port wine. It was always stuffy and stank of perfume and sandalwood hair pomade. This music room had nothing else to recommend it.

She wondered what was above the yellow roses. She darted up the nearest staircase, which happened to be the servants' stairs.

It chafed George's dignity to follow her, even in an empty house. Earls did not take servants' stairs.

The yellow roses climbed up to a guest chamber, decorated in mint green. Elegant but unremarkable. Except for the stars painted on the ceiling and a crescent moon.

The moon keep you, little lark.

She broke into a run.

"This is undignified," George huffed behind her. The footman stayed close, in case she tried to escape.

Above the moon was the nursery. What had once been her bedroom. Sheets had been laid over everything, from the wooden horse to the dollhouse and the crib. It lent the space an air of melancholy, as if it was holding its breath. Waiting. A mobile of crystal drops still hung, catching the light, throwing little rainbows.

It hung from the mouth of a smiling sun painted on the ceiling.

The sun keep you, little lark.

She would bet her favorite pistol that the painted moon was directly below. And in between, her crib, also decorated with larks. She pushed it out of the way. She kicked the carpet away.

Underneath, carved on a very plain floorboard, a tiny lark with a rose in its beak.

George shoved her out of the way. "Pull it up!"

The footman used an iron fire poker to smash at the floor until splinters flew. Tessa wanted to know what was beneath it. What the lullaby meant.

But she wanted to get the hell away from them more. She took one step back, very carefully.

The footman lifted a small strongbox from under the floor. It was thick with dust. It had a lock made of iron, but the rest was wood, too long neglected. It cracked under another blow from the poker. George grabbed at the parchment inside.

Tessa frowned as she continued to edge away. All of this for a letter? George did not notice. He was too intent on his triumph.

The footman, unfortunately, noticed.

He grabbed Tessa's hair, yanking her back. Pain lanced through her skull. She staggered, clawing at his wrist.

But not before she'd glimpsed the writing, the signature, the words.

"Where are you going, lovey?" the footman snarled.

And then an answer, in a voice she had never heard before, all earthquakes and lightning, sword and dagger:

"Get your hands off my wife."

SHE HAD NO idea how Roarke had found her. How he had even known how to begin looking. She was sure of one thing, though.

He was absolutely going to commit murder.

The terrifying giant that the *ton* whispered about was here. And he was as terrifying as they claimed. George had already raced down the long nursery room and out the other door. He knew full well that Roarke could not chase him without abandoning her. And she knew in her bones that he would never abandon her. She wanted to throw herself at him. He'd catch her.

The footman was a problem. He was used to intimidating people who could not fight back. Who weren't as strong as he was, or weren't as cruel. He didn't know what to do with Roarke.

Or with Tessa, for that matter.

She wasn't weeping or begging. She was fuming. Also immobilized, though it galled her to admit it. He might be stronger and meaner, but she was faster. And smarter.

And Roarke was a force of nature.

The thrill that went through her at the look on his face, formidable and relentless, was hot and liquid. And rather badly timed.

"For every second your hands remain on my wife," Roarke said, dark and deadly, "I break another one of your bones."

"If I let her go now, you'll kill me." The footman jerked her back, and she made a little sound of pain. The pressure on her scalp made her eyes water.

"She cries, you die," Roarke said.

The threat rippled through the footman. He knew truth when he heard it.

As it happened, Roarke was tired of waiting.

So was Tessa.

She wasn't quite as steady on her feet as she would have liked, due to the lingering effects of the laudanum, but it didn't stop her. She called on the Tessa she had created for everyone else: flighty, bubbly, cheerful. *That* Tessa had never dealt with a man like the footman, had never known anything but champagne flutes and silk dancing slippers.

That Tessa would surely faint in such a predicament.

She let herself go limp. Abruptly. Heavily.

When he shifted to catch her weight and alter his hold, she rammed her elbow into his groin as hard as she possibly could.

Turned out, elbows were very hard. Sharp.

A satisfying, choked grunt of pain was her reward. His fingers loosened as he doubled over. And then she was suddenly shoved behind Roarke, barely able to see around the breadth of him as he pummeled the footman's face.

Unlike Lord Beville, the footman knew how to fight back and knew how to fight dirty.

It only made Roarke smile, once, as he ducked a vicious return jab. He followed with a strike to the ribs, then the throat. The footman staggered and hit the ground, groaning. Roarke did not stop.

"Roarke," Tessa said. "It's not that I don't appreciate this, but if you murder him, there will be a trial and a lot of fuss."

Another punch.

"You'll have to deal with many, *many* people. All that polite conversation. And you'll definitely have to wear a cravat."

The next punch hovered.

"I'd rather go home," she added. "Wouldn't you?"

Roarke pushed to his feet, sighing. "With you? Always."

The footman cursed, spitting blood. His left eye was already swelling. "Bitch."

Roarke turned, stepping on the man's hand. "This is the hand that touched her," he said quietly. Bones cracked. The footman howled. "Never again."

LENNOX AND FERGUS met them on the stairs.

"Thank God," Lennox said, spotting Tessa unharmed. He said nothing about the blood on Roarke's shirt. Fergus grunted in approval.

"There's a footman in the nursery," Roarke said. "See him to a magistrate or a constable, would you? He had his hands on my wife. No need to be gentle."

The men's faces darkened. Tessa smiled brightly. "I'm perfectly well."

"We'll see to it," Fergus promised.

Roarke tucked Tessa into his side, as if she was going to be stolen again. His jaw was starting to look as if it hurt. She let herself soften against him, suddenly exhausted and yet still feeling as though her blood was pumping too fast. "How did you even find me?"

"Rue found your letter." He glared down at her. *"Rue."*

"That's good, isn't it?"

"*Rue*. Not me."

"Ah."

"We'll be discussing that later, I assure you."

The thrill the stern promise sent through her was very nearly indecent. Heat rushed into her belly. He narrowed his eyes at her warningly.

It did not douse the fire.

Quite the opposite.

"You are incorrigible," he said softly. "Little devil."

He didn't say anything else until they had reached the ground floor, but his hand was warm on her lower back. "What is this place? Why did he bring you here?"

Tessa touched one of the gold birdcages hanging from the

ceiling. "This was my mother's house. Lark House."

He frowned. "Why aren't you living here instead of in that deathtrap?"

"I like that deathtrap," she pointed out tartly. "And I'd forgotten about this house. I haven't been here since I was very little." She climbed into the carriage, waving at Atticus, who waited with a glower and a cudgel in hand. *Not* very subtle. "Did you see George?"

"Aye," Atticus replied. "Jumped into a carriage as though his arse was on fire."

"Follow him. Please."

"Why does George care about the house?" Roarke asked as Atticus pulled into the street traffic.

"Because it's mine," she said darkly. "I saw the papers he stole. It was her dowry, and it's my inheritance. My father put it in trust."

"And your cousin wants to keep it. Why now?"

"I don't know."

Roarke tilted her chin up to inspect her face, her eyes, making sure she was truly unharmed. "Your pupils are a bit dilated."

"He dosed me with laudanum."

Roarke stilled. "I really will kill him."

"It's done."

"Tessa."

She shrugged. "How did you even know it was him that snatched me? I didn't put that in the letter, nor where I was meeting him. I didn't even know it at the time."

He growled. "Another thing we shall discuss. You warned everyone to hide, to be on guard."

"Of course I did."

"And you never once considered being on guard yourself?" he ground out.

"I had my daggers." It was a feeble excuse, and she knew it. "How did you find me?" she asked again, softly.

"I found Paulette packing her things in a haste."

She blinked. "Paulette? Who weeps at every provocation and fainted when she found a spider? *That* Paulette?"

"The very one."

"Not a frightened maid, then?"

"Definitely not."

"She used my own trick against me!" She was outraged. She ought to have seen through the subterfuge. It had been her entire life at one time, after all.

"George sent her," he said, still stroking her cheek. Tessa did the mental calculations, noting the evidence of unlocked windows, of weasels pawing through belongings in a most un-weasel-like way. They'd assumed it was someone after one of the others. Not her. No one had bothered with her since she ran away, since The Incident, and barely even before then. "She confessed. Eventually."

Tessa's eyes widened at the unspoken implications of that statement and its dry delivery. "What did Rue do to her?"

"You don't want to know. And it was not nearly as vicious as what Bryony did."

"Bryony?"

"Your army rose to the call, devil."

She swallowed. "For me?"

"For you." He kissed her lightly. "Don't you know by now that I'd do anything for you?"

The kiss went deep, demanding. He stole her breath. Her very thoughts. It was a nice reprieve, however short. It fueled her, grounded her. How did he manage that, even now? To make her feel calm and safe and messy and wonderfully wild?

Atticus knocked on the carriage ceiling. "I've got him."

They pulled apart, glancing out the window. They'd left Bath proper, and the road cut through fields and trees, blurring as the horses gave chase. Tessa craned her neck to get a better look and heard the clatter of wheels, horses snorting. The wind in her face. Dirt and pebbles kicked up against the carriage. Roarke drew her back inside. "Have a care."

The horses slowed. Tessa sat up straighter. "What's happening? Is he getting away?"

The carriage wobbled to a stop.

"We'll never catch him now!"

"Just wait," Roarke said, pushing the door open. She jumped down after him, not waiting for assistance. He clucked his tongue at her disapprovingly. She stuck hers right out at him in response.

The sun was warm on her head as she hurried into the road. George's carriage was racing ahead. He was getting away. He was getting *away*.

Roarke looked just as calm, as confident, as always.

This was not the time for calm confidence, damnation.

And then up ahead, just before the road turned, a rider stepped out, blocking the way.

George's coachman shouted and pulled on the reins. The carriage veered, teetered sideways on two wheels, then righted itself with a loud crack. The horses stopped, tossing their heads.

Rue sat perched on Tessa's horse. On either side of the road, Tessa glimpsed Daphne and Bryony. Bryony had left the safety of Magpie House. For her. She was pale, like a vengeful ghost, the lower half of her face hidden behind a scrap of cloth. George stumbled out of the carriage, glowering and shouting.

A knife embedded itself in the carriage door beside his shoulder.

Tessa nearly cheered.

"You're the highwaywoman," Roarke said. "They're waiting for you. Have at it."

She beamed at him, speechless. Had there ever been such a man?

And then he handed her a pistol. It was clearly the best quality, made just for her, with a bird inlaid on the handle. "Go on, then."

"I love you," she blurted out.

It wasn't the right time for such declarations. But if you couldn't tell your husband you loved him when were a bit drug-addled and he was arming you for crime, when could you tell him?

"Yet another thing we shall discuss," he promised roughly. He grabbed her chin, kissed her hard. "At great length."

She strode away, feeling his eyes on her. He fell into step behind her before she'd reached her cousin. She'd hardly expected differently. Roarke might arm her, but he would never let her go alone. Wouldn't let her go at all. She clung to that hope. Something for later. A possibility? Or a delusion?

"What is the meaning of this?" George sputtered.

"Stand and deliver," Rue declared with satisfying menace.

"You're robbing me?" he gaped. "Preposterous. Do you know who I am?"

"A thief?" Tessa suggested.

He whirled, finally noticing her. His eyes bulged when Roarke pinned him with a cold glare that suggested a great deal of pain was in store.

"What are you doing here? What is this?" George took a step in her direction. "Stop this at once."

She lifted her pistol. He froze. "I believe you were in the process of being robbed."

He fumed, turning red.

"Hand it over," Tessa said.

"Now," Roarke snapped when George hesitated.

"You won't shoot me," George said.

Tessa shrugged. "I don't know if I would," she admitted. "But he would." Roarke folded his arms. "And she definitely would." Rue smiled. It was not comforting.

"I know all of your real names," George said.

"See, that just makes me want to shoot you more," Rue remarked. "Not very bright, is he?"

"You've already forgotten their names," Roarke said. "And any secrets you might know. In fact, you will make sure they are all safe in their new lives. Because if anything happens to any of them, I'll come for you." He advanced, plucking the knife from the carriage door. "And I don't miss."

"You're a disgrace," George said.

"Yes." Tessa rolled her eyes. "That's the point. You really are an idiot, aren't you?" She marched forward and pulled the crumpled parchment from his pocket. "I believe this is mine."

When George twitched in protest, Roarke shoved him back. He stumbled, yelping.

"You could have done this at any time over the years," Tessa pointed out, reading the will, the faded and brown ink. The signature in her father's handwriting.

"I couldn't find the bloody will, now could I? And then your bloody giant of a husband started talking to lawyers and setting up house trusts and making inquiries about women inheriting, I knew it was a matter of time."

She looked up. "Yes, you've been through such a trial," she said blandly. Roarke had been making sure Magpie House stayed in her hands, even after marriage. George did not need to know that. "Poor you."

Roarke's lips twitched in a brief smile. He glanced over her shoulder at the will. "It appears you own a second house. Congratulations."

Her father had not forgotten her after all. Had not abandoned her to his careless and greedy family.

"Right," Rue announced. "I've had enough of this one's face." She poked George with the end of her musket. "Off you go."

"*What?*"

"I'm keeping your carriage. Your coachman can do as he likes, I suppose. As long as he does not make of himself a nuisance."

Daphne laughed as she strolled out of the greenery. "Splendid. It would have been a long walk home."

Tessa rolled the parchment carefully. "All this for a house in Bath when he already has a fortune."

"Some people are never satisfied," Roarke said.

She wanted to ask him if he was, but didn't. She wavered a bit on her feet. He caught her. "I'm still a bit fuzzy," she admitted.

"Let's get you home." He turned to help her back to the carriage, where Atticus waited, still holding his cudgel. George was muttering furiously. She caught a flash of him as he raced into the bushes.

"Is he… in his smalls?"

"Yes," Rue said. "I've stolen his clothes. He didn't deserve them."

Tessa smiled. She felt like she might burst with the joy snaking through the chaos of the day. "You came for me," she said. "All of you."

"Of course we came for you," Rue replied. She huffed at the genuine surprise on Tessa's face. "Now who's the idiot?

Chapter Twenty-Five

TESSA WOKE TO a quiet house. Even Parsley was sleeping peacefully. She felt herself again, the laudanum having passed through her system, leaving only a deep thirst and the kind of hunger that rumbled like thunder. She tiptoed out of the chambers, on the hunt for something to eat.

Roarke's door swung open instantly. "Where are you going?"

She started, hand flying to her racing heart. "Roarke."

"Running away?" His face was cast in shadows, dark, hard. But she knew it was hurt that lurked beneath the clipped question. She could soothe him, flatter him. But that was the old Tessa, and he had never smiled at that Tessa the way he smiled at the one who tried to steal his carriage in a rainstorm.

"I'm looking for scones," she said instead. It threw him off slightly, as intended. The hurt softened. Something like amusement flared instead, though he did not smile. "With blackberries. I'm hungry."

He stepped into the hall, wearing only his dressing gown. She could see a good portion of his chest, his tanned skin. "You slept through dinner."

"What time is it?" She wondered if her father's pocket watch was fixable.

"Half past two."

"I slept for more than ten hours?"

"Laudanum can do that to a person." His jaw clenched as he fell into step beside her.

The kitchen was dark and quiet, the tables scrubbed clean. A bowl of apples and pears sat beside a covered plate of scones. Tessa snatched one up immediately, her stomach rumbling. Roarke poured her a glass of apple cider and rummaged for a bowl of clotted cream. He broke a scone in half, slathering it with jam and cream. She couldn't stop watching his hands, the flex of his tendons at the wrist. His forearms were more than twice the size of other men's.

He lifted the morsel of scone to her mouth, waiting for her lips to part. She licked the pad of his thumb, catching the last bit of blackberry jam. His eyes narrowed on her, utterly focused. She swallowed, suddenly feeling naked. She may as well have been eating pastries in her bare bottom, the cool night air on her nipples. Everything went hot and liquid.

Roarke leaned closer, edging into her space until he was all she could see. "We have things to discuss," he said silkily, with a touch of menace. The kind that made her press her thighs together. She tried to nip at his bottom lip, but he eased away, just enough.

Denied, her desire curled tighter and hotter. As did his. She could see it in the way his breath changed, the way he watched her mouth. She wanted to tell him that she loved him again. But he had not said it back. There was no guarantee that he did not wish things to remain as they were. She had not exactly brought quiet and peace to his life.

Why was this scarier than Lord Beville's dagger at her throat, the footman grabbing at her? This should be easy. Simple, at least.

"Roarke," she breathed. "I need you."

It was truth.

But only part of the truth.

His eyes narrowed further. She licked her bottom lip. He tracked the movement. She played with the ribbon holding the neckline of her nightdress together. One little tug and it would fall to the ground at her feet.

"Tessa." It was a warning. A delicious warning.

"If you won't undress me," she replied, "I suppose I must do it myself."

She undid the knot. He growled. The sound filled her with light and heat. Her nightdress slid to the stones. His frown was scolding, chiding, but his hands were already on her. They stroked up her sides, under her breasts, ever so faintly over her nipples. She arched closer. He bent his head to suck one into his mouth, flicking at her with his hot tongue. She moaned. Loudly. Wantonly. Naked in her kitchen.

He trailed his fingers between her thighs, beside her sex. Her bud felt swollen as it throbbed. He circled it once with his thumb, filling her with two fingers, suddenly, perfectly. She tightened around him, so he did it again. And again.

Stopped.

"Roarke," she begged, her release just out of her grasp. So close, so very close.

"Not until *you* stop running away from me."

"I'm right here." She tried to get closer, to rub her folds over his hardness. She reached for him, frantic to feel his cock, to make him want her as much as she wanted him. For him to beg. He was so hard, so smooth. His hands around her upper arms held her still. Frustrated, she made a sound she had never made before. He smiled. She glared at him. "Do you think this is funny?"

"I could cry with the need to bury myself inside of you," he said roughly. "To take you so deeply, to fill you so completely, there's nowhere for you to go."

"Then do it!" His words brought that release close again, teasing with her. "*Now*. If you really want me."

And that was the question, wasn't it? The seed of doubt despite it all.

"You're my wife," he growled in her ear. Shivers trailed along her neck like tiny bites. "More than that, you are Tessa. And I will always want you."

Oh, how she wanted to believe him. Wanted it so desperately. Desperate enough to be brave. Reckless. "You chose me because you could leave me," she reminded him.

His fingers tightened on her. "Is that what you think?"

"It's what we agreed on."

"Tessa." He lifted her chin when she would not meet his gaze. Could not. "I chose *you* because I didn't *want* to leave you."

Her breath wavered.

He cursed under his breath. She was still naked in his arms. Vulnerable. Powerful.

Surely this was worth fighting for. She did not move, did not give in to the urge to run.

"I promised to stay away to keep you safe."

She frowned. "From what?"

"Me."

"Not that again."

"I'm the Beast of the Dartmoor."

She wriggled against him temptingly. "I have met true beasts, Roarke. You were never one."

"I would never forgive myself if I dimmed your light. The way Lara's dimmed."

"You didn't dim her light," Tessa argued. "She was unhappy. Sheltered—I daresay spoiled. And it suited her to make you the monster. That's what the *ton* does, after all."

"I scared her."

"You don't scare *me*."

"So that's that?" A flicker of amusement again, through the devastating guilt he had carried too long.

"That's that," she said firmly.

He kissed her lightly. "I tried to stay away."

"So did I."

"I'm aware," he returned drily. "Don't run from me, Tessa. If you want to leave, say so."

She hooked her leg around his hip, lifting her soft, wet center to his, pushing against this cock until it slid between her folds. "I don't want to leave."

"Devil." The soft tone of it, the affectionate pinch of her bottom, made the love she felt even brighter. Made it into something she did not fear. How could she? It was Roarke. It would always be Roarke.

"I'll always come for you," he said against her throat. "Always. And I will never, ever let anyone take your sparkle."

She lifted her other leg, and he fit himself against her, lifting her up so her bottom filled his hands. "Now," she said, as he thrust up inside her. *"Now."*

"Now," he promised, filling her again and again, holding her tight against his body. "Always."

They moved against each other, hard, fast, desperate. Her release came for her, tightening her inner core, slowly at first, then building.

"Tessa?" Roarke rasped in her ear.

"Yes?" she moaned on another spasm of pleasure.

"Start counting."

Epilogue

THE *TON* STILL did not quite know what to make of the Countess of Dartmoor.

The Incident seemed nothing compared to stories of runaway heiresses, abductions, and decrepit houses where the chandelier might knock you on your arse if you were not invited.

It did not know what to make of the Beast of Dartmoor, either.

He was just as silent, just as intimidating, but anyone could see he loved his wife to distraction. And their baby girl, Deirdre Rose Noble, whose first words were "Stand and Deliver!"—shouted at a footman passing by with a tray of fresh blackberry scones. Tessa adored her little ragamuffin. She had *not* adored the experience of being pregnant, it had to be said.

They rarely went to London, despite the many invitations, though they sometimes traveled to Lark House, where Tessa held balls that involved acrobats and fire eating, care of Lord Kensington. Using her old debutante skills, she also held firework nights, footraces for women who usually eschewed grass stains and sunburned noses, and romps through the parks where she pointed out all of the birds. All for a price of admission. That price, which was exorbitant, went to the care of the women she hid in the country. And when his wife hosted a ball or an event of any kind, Roarke was there, moving through the crowd, less as a host and more as a threat.

Mrs. Pompadour took over the running of Lark House, and Rue stepped into her role at Magpie House, safely ensconced with Holly and Fergus. No one mentioned the chambers they all shared, or the fond touches that passed between them. Magpie House was a safe house, and always would be.

Bryony moved into the dower house, preferring the solitude. A castle with a moat full of alligators and a garden of bears would have been less impenetrable. But she left little gifts at the main house, bunches of wildflowers, a cake decorated with violets. A knife with a magpie painted on the blade. A dictionary of poison plants.

Daphne moved back to London, where every door opened to her, care of threatening letters sent by Roarke before her arrival. He was getting rather good at them. They sent a chill through the blood without any clear evidence of a tangible threat.

Magpie convinced Noni to take her on as an apprentice of sorts. She was voracious for knowledge, especially midwifery. She stayed at Magpie House, on hand when needed.

More women arrived, led by word of mouth, by whispers in the retiring rooms at balls, and stories told behind painted fans at tea. No one dared approach Magpie House and its army of footmen, its traps hidden in the grass and between the trees. Not earls, not viscounts, not dukes.

Only the Beast of Dartmoor.

Tessa waited impatiently at the end of the drive for just that. She'd take a beast over an earl any day. *Her* beast.

He'd been gone two weeks now, to London for a dreaded speech in the House of Lords and then a round of threats to men who needed threatening. She had opted to stay home so he might return sooner. Little Deirdre, currently up at the house chasing Lennox with a tiny wooden sword, did not make traveling easy. And London was not ready for her. Might never be. Tessa rather prided herself on that.

When the carriage trundled into view, excitement leapt in her chest. *Finally.*

Atticus reined in the horses long enough for Roarke to step out and then continue onward to the stables. He stalked toward Tessa, eyes devouring her. "Three weeks is too long," he said. "We're not doing that again."

"Good."

"What did I miss?" he asked, closing the last of the distance that separated them.

"Deidre is the Queen of the Pirates this week. She's drowned entire battalions in the pond and perfected her bloodcurdling battle shriek."

"Of course she did." He was proud as ten peacocks.

"The rooster took it as a challenge."

He laughed.

"It has not been quiet."

"And you? What did you do?"

"I was the very picture of ladylike decorum."

He shuddered. "Don't threaten me."

He caught her up against his solid chest, and her toes left the ground. The kiss was soft, a teasing nip, a drink on a soft summer night, but his hands were hard and hungry as they roamed her back, clasped the back of her neck. The perfect contradiction. She moaned into his mouth, and his fingers tightened. "I don't like this dress," he muttered.

She pulled back, mildly offended. It was brand new, not a torn hem or slipped stitch to be seen. Not a single dust mark. "What? Why not?"

"There's far too much of it."

She nipped at his bottom lip. He growled, just a little. Especially when she squirmed free and stepped back, grinning. "You can run," he whispered in her ear, teasing, tempting. It was their game, their promise to each other. Running or chasing, she always, always felt chosen. *They* always felt chosen. "But I'll always catch you."

She tossed a grin over her shoulder. "Prove it."

And then she raced into the trees, bright laughter trailing behind her.

"Little devil," he murmured, slowly loosening his cravat as he followed.

About the Author

Alyxandra Harvey lives in an old stone house with her husband, multiple dogs, and a few resident ghosts who are allowed to stay as long as they keep company manners. She likes chai lattes, tattoos, and books. Sometimes fueled by literary rage.

Author of The Drake Chronicles, The Witches of London, Haunting Violet, Red, Love Me Love Me Not.

Twitter: AlyxandraH
Instagram: alyxandraharveyauthor

www.ingramcontent.com/pod-product-compliance
Lightning Source LLC
Chambersburg PA
CBHW070345200726
48294CB00003B/792

* 9 7 8 1 9 6 1 2 7 5 6 1 4 *